A THOUSAND Cuts

CELL BLOCK C
MELISSA TOPPEN

Copyright © 2020 by Melissa Toppen

All rights reserved. Except as permitted by U.S. Copyright Act of 1976, no part of this publication may be reproduced, distributed, or transmitted in any form or by any means, or stored in a database or retrieval system, without prior permission of the author.

The scanning, uploading, and distribution of this book via the Internet or via other means without the permission of the publisher is illegal and punishable by law. Please purchase only authorized electronic editions and do not participate in or encourage electronic piracy of copyrighted materials.

This book is a work of fiction. Names, characters, establishments, or organizations, and incidents are either products of the author's imagination or are used fictitiously to give a sense of authenticity. Any resemblance to actual persons, living or dead, events, or locales is entirely coincidental. This book is intended for 18+ older, and for mature audiences only.

Editing by Amy Gamache @ Rose David Editing

Cover Design by Sly Fox Cover Designs

Table of Contents

Chapter 1	9
Chapter 2	22
Chapter 3	29
Chapter 4	38
Chapter 5	55
Chapter 6	64
Chapter 7	70
Chapter 8	86
Chapter 9	100
Chapter 10	120
Chapter 11	128
Chapter 12	142
Chapter 13	158
Chapter 14	172
Chapter 15	189
Chapter 16	202
Chapter 17	216
Chapter 18	220
Chapter 19	237
Chapter 20	251
Chapter 21	264
Chapter 22	276
Chapter 23	285
Chapter 24	291
Chapter 25	300
Chapter 26	313
Chapter 27	322
Epilogue	329

Chapter 1

Ainsley

"Hey, Ains, you home?" my brother, Finn calls down the hallway, his voice filtering through the open doorway of my bedroom.

"Yeah. I'm back here," I holler back, sorting through the pile of clothes stacked on top of my bed.

The last thing I want to be doing on a Friday night is laundry, but between work and school, I have to fit it in whenever I can.

"I stopped and got pizza on the way home." His tall frame appears in the doorway moments later, a square box from Maggiano's in his hands. "Ham and pineapple, your favorite." He gives me a toothy grin. "I hope you're hungry."

"Starving, actually. I haven't eaten anything since the granola bar I scarfed down between my Human Behaviors and Political Science classes this afternoon."

"You need to make time to eat." He gives me the same look our dad used to give us whenever he was concerned about something.

"I do make time to eat. But Fridays are my busiest days and sometimes it slips my mind."

"You work too hard. All I ever see you do is study, go to class, and go to work. You're only twenty, Ains. You should be out enjoying life a little."

"It's not like I have much of a choice. I have to keep my GPA up so I don't lose my financial aid, and I have to work to pay for what my financial aid doesn't cover. Maybe one day I'll have the luxury of *me* time, but clearly right now is not it," I huff.

"Well, I'm sure the laundry can wait for a few minutes while you eat, yeah?" He looks at the half-folded pile of clothes in front of me before his brown eyes dart back up to my face.

"Normally, I would say no." I smile. "But you know I can't resist a pineapple pizza from Maggiano's."

"Well come on." He jerks his chin upward before spinning around and disappearing down the hallway.

I immediately abandon my laundry and follow after him.

When I enter the living room, Finn is coming out of the kitchen with a can of Coke in each hand. Extending one to me as he passes, he takes the far end of the worn-down leather couch while I take the other, the pizza box between us.

Leaning forward, I set my drink on the coffee table before lifting the top of the pizza box up and grabbing a slice.

Even though we have a table in our kitchen, we rarely ever eat at it. Sometimes in the mornings, if I have time for a bowl of cereal, I will sit in there, but for the most part we always eat in the living room in front of the television. That's how it was when our dad was alive and that's how it's remained.

"So," Finn grabs a piece of pizza and takes a huge bite, "how was school today?" he asks around his mouth full of food.

"It was good. I'll be glad when this semester is over. My course load is ridiculous. It wouldn't be so bad if I had some BS classes but every single one I'm taking is hard."

"Whose fault is that?" He arches a brow at me as he tears another bite off with his teeth. "Maybe if you weren't so hell bent on finishing your degree in three years, you could afford to take less classes."

"But the sooner I finish school, the sooner I can stop waitressing and start making some real money. I can't live here with you forever."

"Why not?"

"Why not?" I look around the room, taking in the faded walls and worn carpet.

"It's not that bad." He reads my expression. "Beyond the fact that it's paid off, this is where we grew up. Where every memory we have is. Our grandpa built this house, for crying out loud."

"Yeah, like a hundred years ago." I take another bite of pizza. "But that wasn't my point."

"Then what *is* your point?" He smiles, causing the sides of his eyes to crinkle.

Finn looks so much like our dad sometimes it's unsettling. Same tall stature. Same broad shoulders. Same dark hair and eyes. Same deep laugh. Finn even rocks the two-day old scruff the way he used to.

It's uncanny.

Me, on the other hand, I look nothing like our father, with the exception of my dark hair. I've got our mother's green eyes and petite features. Not that I actually remember what she looked like, considering she left when I was a toddler. But I have a couple old pictures that my dad gave me when I was younger and the resemblance between the two of us is undeniable. Kind of like Dad and Finn.

"Well," I comment after swallowing the bite in my mouth. "I would like to get married and have a family of my own one day. I don't think living with my big bro is really conducive to that."

"I don't know. I think my future nieces and nephews would love to live with their Uncle Finn."

"You're funny." I roll my eyes at him. "But *no*."

As much as I love my brother, I can't wait for the day that I can afford to move out on my own. It's nothing against him. He's done more for me than any older brother should ever have to do. But there comes a time in every person's life where they crave a certain level of independence.

I want that for myself, but I also want it for Finn. He deserves to be able to live his life for him, not me. And that's something he hasn't been able to do since our dad passed away eight years ago. Most eighteen-year-old's likely wouldn't want the responsibility of raising their kid sister, but Finn didn't hesitate.

He had to become the man of the house overnight. He's worked two, sometimes three jobs, for as long as I can remember. And if he had any aspirations of going to college, he shelved them because he knew there was no way he could take care of me, work, and go to school. Of course, I started helping as much as I could soon as I as was old enough. And while I don't contribute much, every little bit helps.

I tried to get a full-time job right out of high school, but Finn insisted that I focus on school. He really is the most incredible brother in the world, even if he does drive me crazy most of the time. I have no idea where I'd be without him.

He says I'm this family's future. That I'm the one that was destined for something more. More than this old, run down ranch. More than this less than desirable neighborhood. More than the life Finn seems to think isn't good enough for me.

I wish he could see that he's always given me everything I've needed. Even if we can't afford the finer things in life, we've always had enough to get by and that's enough for me.

Once the pizza is nearly gone, Finn breaks the silence that has fallen between us. "So, while we're both here, I have something I need to talk to you about." He turns toward me, tucking one of his legs under the other.

"Okay," I draw out, waiting for him to continue.

"I got a phone call today and…" A knock at the door cuts him off midsentence and both of our gazes swing toward the front of the house. Finn makes no attempt to get up.

"You going to get that?" I ask, not surprised by the interruption. It's not uncommon for one of Finn's buddies to show up unannounced, especially on the weekends.

"In a minute." His focus comes back to me. "As I was saying…" Again, he's interrupted by another loud knock.

"Let me just get it." I push to my feet and quickly cross the living room.

"Ains, wait." Finn attempts to stop me but it's too late. I already have my hand on the knob and am tugging the door open before he can reach me.

I don't understand why Finn didn't want me to get the door. That is until my eyes land on the absolute last person I ever expected to see standing on my front porch again… Ryland Thorpe.

A million memories slam into me. One after the other in quick succession.

Ryland sleeping on my floor two nights in a row when I was nine after I swore there was something living in my closet. Him walking me to my first day of Junior High to make sure no one messed with me. The tree we used to climb in my backyard before we had to tear it down. How we would sit on those branches for hours talking. Him holding me the night my father died. Him promising me that he would always be there for me.

Him breaking every promise he ever made. Betraying me in a way I never thought he would.

Him going to jail. Him almost taking my brother down with him…

He has a lot of nerve showing his face here after everything he's done. Yet, it doesn't stop my heart from picking up speed the way it always used to whenever he would walk into a room.

Ryland's even more handsome than I remembered. Then again, I was fifteen the last time I saw him.

He's always had an amazing build, but he looks even bulkier now. His biceps strain against the fabric of his white t-shirt. His hair now shorter than it used to be, trimmed close to his scalp on the sides while the top is slightly longer and pushed back from his face.

He looks good, too good for someone who has spent the last five years in prison. Which brings me back to why I'm so completely thrown to see him here.

"What the…" I draw back, confusion clear on my face as his gray eyes lock with mine.

"Hi, Ainsley." Ryland gives me a tentative smile, shuffling his weight from one foot to the other. "God, look at you. You're all grown up."

The way he looks at me causes every nerve ending in my body to spark to life.

"What are you doing here?" I shake my head in an effort to break the fog that seems to have settled around me.

"I thought we were meeting up in the morning." Finn appears at my side.

"Yeah, well…" Ryland hesitates.

"I take it the visit with your mom didn't go so well?" Finn guesses.

"I think it's safe to say that relationship is dead. I don't think I'll be going back there again."

"I tried to tell you."

"I know." Ryland blows out a breath, the action drawing my gaze to his lips. *God, those lips.* I quickly shake off the thought. "I didn't want to put you out so I called a cab. I'm hoping your offer's still good for a place to crash." Ryland holds up the small duffle clutched in his right hand.

My gaze whips to my brother. I'm seconds away from stating the obvious — that this man nearly landed him in prison right alongside him. But before I can form a single word, Finn looks down at me, his expression soft.

"Of course." His words are meant for Ryland but his eyes are on me.

"That's what you wanted to talk to me about?" I say instead of voicing my thoughts. "That's why you brought me home my favorite pizza. You thought you could butter me up."

"Ainsley." Finn's brows furrow.

"Don't Ainsley me," I hiss, taking a step back. "He can't stay here." I gesture toward the doorway, making it a point not to look at Ryland.

"He can and he is. He's going to stay in Dad's old room until he can get himself sorted out."

"Have you lost your mind?" I draw back. "He's a convicted felon."

"I'm aware." Finn remains completely calm which only serves to piss me off more. "But he's served his time. And he's family."

"*Family*?" I snort. "He was selling drugs! *Drugs*, Finn. Do I need to remind you why our mother left?" My voice shakes. "And clearly I *do* need to remind you that he almost took you down with him. Why would you agree to this without talking to me? You knew I wouldn't be okay with this."

"I know. But there are things you don't know." Finn sighs, running a hand through his hair.

"Like what? What don't I know?" I tap my foot impatiently.

"Can we talk about this later?" His gaze slides to Ryland before coming back to me.

"If he's staying here, then I'm not."

"Don't be ridiculous. This is Ryland. You've known him your entire life."

"I *thought* I knew him," I correct. "Obviously I was wrong."

"It's fine," Ryland injects, pulling our attention to him. "Clearly this wasn't a good idea." He nods at Finn. "I'll figure something else out." He starts to back away.

"He has nowhere else to go, Ains." Finn pulls me out of the doorway and back into the living room. "I know you don't trust him, but I do. He deserves a second chance, more than most people do. Can you please, *please*, just trust me on this?"

I study my brother for a long moment. Even though I want to stomp my foot like a spoiled toddler and refuse to agree, I also know that when Finn is this adamant about something, there's usually a good reason.

I suck in a deep breath. The last thing I want to do is agree to let Ryland Thorpe stay here, especially after everything that happened five years ago. But the look on my brother's face tells me that I really don't have a say in the matter. He just wants me to believe that I do. Typical Finn.

"Fine," I grumble, crossing my arms in front of my chest. "But if you think I'm going to forget what he almost did to you, *to us*, I'm not."

"That's fair." Finn smiles. "Thanks, kid." He nudges my shoulder before heading back to the front door.

Spinning on my heel, I make a beeline for my room, slamming the door the moment I'm inside. Pacing back and forth, I'm not sure if I want to scream or cry. Both feel like pretty good options right about now.

Seven years. That's how long Ryland was sentenced for his drug trafficking conviction. I remember that day like it was yesterday. Sitting in that courtroom, both furious with Ryland and terrified for him at the same time. When they read the sentencing, stating he was given the maximum for his crimes, I wasn't sure if I was relieved or devastated. Maybe I was both.

All I know for sure is that my life changed forever that day. I had to say goodbye to the girl I was. The girl who believed in silly fairy tales. The girl who thought one day she would ride off into the sunset with her true love. The girl who believed that Ryland Thorpe was a prince. *Her* prince.

More like a wolf in sheep's clothing.

In that one careless and selfish act, he threatened to take everything from me. I had already lost my mother and father. Then, the one person I thought would never hurt me, almost took my brother away from me. The only family I have left.

I still shudder at the thought of what would have happened had they charged Finn, too. Even if he hadn't done jail time, there's no doubt in my mind that they would have taken me out of his care and I would have ended up in foster care, or worse – a group home.

The fact that Ryland had put me in that position really made me see just how little he actually cared about me. I think that was the hardest part of all; realizing that the person I was secretly in love with didn't feel the same, but that he cared so little he would put my entire life in jeopardy.

And now he's back. After all these years he's here. Only he's not the person I thought I knew. Hell, I'm not sure that he ever was. And while Finn may have chosen to forgive him, I sure as hell haven't.

I haven't forgiven him for the drugs. I haven't forgiven him for putting my brother's future at risk. I haven't forgiven him for leading me to believe he was someone else. But most of all, I haven't forgiven him for breaking my heart.

Chapter 2

Ainsley

Eight years ago...
"*Hey, kid.*" *Ryland smiles as he enters my room, flopping down on the side of my bed moments later. "What are you reading?" He gestures to the book in my hand.*

"*Tiger's Curse.*" *I hold the book up so he can get a good look at the cover.*

"*Tiger's Curse, huh? What's that about?*"

"*It's about a guy who's been cursed to live as a tiger for three hundred years by an evil king and now a girl is trying to help him break the curse. I'm not very far yet, but I really like it.*"

"*Cursed to live as a tiger?*" *He cocks a brow at me.*

"*It's kind of like* Beauty and the Beast.*" I use a comparison I know he'll get. Everyone knows* Beauty and the Beast.

"*Ahhh, gotcha.*" *He nods.*

"*Did you need something?*" *I ask, laying the book face down on the mattress.*

"*No, I just wanted to check in. See how my favorite girl is doing.*" *He grins.*

"I'm okay." *I pick at a loose thread on the blanket that's thrown over my lap.*

If I had a dime for every time someone has asked me that over the last two weeks…

"Hey." *Ryland places his hand on my shin, pulling my gaze back to him.* *"It's me. If you're not okay, you know you can tell me, right?"*

"I know." *I blow out a breath.* *"I miss my dad,"* *I admit, tears immediately building behind my eyes.*

It's been thirteen days. Thirteen days since I came home from school and found my dad unconscious on the floor. Thirteen days since I watched the paramedics try to revive him. Thirteen days since they failed.

Thirteen days…

I'm trying really hard to be strong. For Finn, for me. I'm trying to pretend like everything is okay. Like I'm not worried about what's going to happen next. Like I didn't just lose my father. Like I might lose my brother if he isn't granted guardianship of me at tomorrow's hearing.

Truth is, I'm barely holding on. I'm scared. Terrified is more like it.

Finn keeps telling me that everything will be okay. That he knows they'll make him my legal guardian and that no one is going to rip us apart, but deep down I know he's worried, too. He's not nearly as good at hiding his feelings as he thinks he is.

That, and he's not very good at making sure his twelve-year-old sister isn't eavesdropping on the multiple conversations he's had regarding the matter.

There's a lot working against him. The fact that he's barely eighteen. The fact that he just graduated high school days ago and only has a part time job, which doesn't supply nearly enough income to provide for himself, let alone his little sister.

Luckily, it looks like we get to keep the house, so at least there's that. Except that's about the only good news we've gotten this week.

Finn is so stressed out. The only thing I can think to do is put on a brave face and not give him more reasons to worry.

"I know you do, kid." Ryland gets up and crosses to the other side of the bed before sliding in next to me. Propping himself up against the headboard, he drapes an arm around my shoulder and pulls me to his side. "We all miss him." He rests his cheek on the top of my head. "But you still have Finn," he reminds me. "And you still have me. And I'm not going anywhere." He gives me a squeeze.

"What if they take me away? What if they don't let me stay here with Finn?" I voice my concern out loud for the first time.

"You can't think like that, Ains. Finn will find a way. One way or another. Your brother will never let anyone take you."

"But what if he can't stop them?"

"Then I guess I'll have to hide you away where no one will be able to find you. Then they can't take you."

"You'd do that?"

"For you, I'd do anything. You're my family, you and Finn. I'll always protect you. You know that, right?"

There isn't a time in my life that I remember without Ryland. He's been my brother's best friend since before I was born and spends more time here than he spends at his own house. I overheard Finn and Dad talking about it one day. How Ryland's stepdad likes to hit him. The thought makes me sick to my stomach.

"Finn's going to win. He's going to convince the judge that you two staying together is the most important thing."

"You mean the three of us," I correct him.

"What?" He pulls back, looking down at me.

"You said the two of us. But it's not just two of us. You are a part of this family, remember?"

"You're right." He smiles and I can't help but think how cute he is.

I've had a crush on Ryland for years. Even when I was little. I'd followed him around in my diapers calling him my boyfriend. Except now things have started to feel differently for me as of late. Maybe it's because I'm getting older. Or maybe it's because I'm starting to understand the feelings I've always secretly harbored for him.

"So, I was thinking, what do you say you and I head down to Apollo's? We could grab some burgers and then stop for ice cream after. How's that sound to you?"

"Is Finn coming, too?"

"No, he has some things he has to take care of before his meeting tomorrow. I thought it would do you some good to get out of this bedroom. You practically never leave your room anymore."

"It's the best place to read." I gesture to the book sitting next to me.

"You read too much." He chuckles.

"You don't read enough," I fire back.

"Well, you're not wrong there." He ruffles a hand through my hair. "So what do you say, you and me, burgers and ice cream?"

"I think that sounds good." I nod, watching Ryland shift before climbing out of the bed.

"Well come on then, my dear Ainsley." He bows his head and extends his hand to me like a man bowing before royalty.

"You're such a dork." I laugh for what feels like the first time in days.

"That's Sir Dork to you." He lifts his face. "Now, are you going to take my hand or what?"

I shake my head, not able to wipe the smile from my face.

"Thank you, Sir Dork." I take his hand, allowing him to help me out of bed. "You know, I've been dying to see that new movie that just came out. The Hunger Games.*"*

"Burgers, ice cream, and a movie. Now you're pushing your luck," Ryland teases.

"I've heard it's really good. I read the book last year."

"Isn't that movie a little mature for someone your age?" He crosses his arms in front of himself.

"Now you sound like Finn." I give him a knowing look. "And for your information, I'm plenty old enough to see it. My dad already said I could." I don't realize what I've said until it's already out. My words hit me like a sledgehammer to the chest.

How easy it is to forget that he's gone.

"I'll tell you what, if there's a decent show time this evening then I'll take you," Ryland concedes, clearly not missing the way my expression had fallen.

"Really?" My mood instantly improves. Not that my sadness really ever lessens but certain things have a way of making it less noticeable.

"Really." He taps the tip of my nose with his index finger. "Now, why don't you get changed?" He looks down at my penguin covered pajamas. "Meet me in the living room when you're ready. I'm going to go tell Finn our plans."

"Okay," I eagerly agree, knowing time with Ryland is exactly what I need right now.

If there's one person in this world that has the ability to make me feel better, Ryland Thorpe is it. A fact he's proven more times than I could ever count over the course of my life.

He is my constant. Him and my brother, Finn. They have always been there for me. My protectors. My support. My family. And now, they're the only ones I have left.

Chapter 3

Ainsley

"Good morning." I jump and let out a startled yelp at the sound of a deep voice behind me.

Turning, my hand goes to my chest, directly over my now pounding heart, as my eyes scan the kitchen. They finally land on Ryland who's sitting at the kitchen table, a cup of coffee in front of him.

"You scared the crap out of me," I scold him, my pulse quickening even more at the sight of him. His hair is rumpled from sleep and he's wearing the same white t-shirt he showed up in last night. Except now it's wrinkled and pulled loose at the neck. He looks incredibly sexy – not that he has the ability to look any other way – but the thought still pisses me off. "Why are you sitting over there in the dark?"

"It's not dark." He gestures around the dimly lit kitchen. The only light is being provided by small slivers of sun peering in through the closed blinds on the back door.

"Um, yeah, it kind of is," I tell him, flipping on the light switch. Unfortunately, we have the worst lighting in our kitchen so it doesn't really offer that much more light.

"There's a fresh pot of coffee," he tells me when I turn, heading toward the refrigerator. "I just made it a few minutes ago."

"I don't drink coffee." I pull open the fridge door before snagging the jug of OJ off the top shelf.

"Gotcha," I hear him mutter but I choose to ignore him.

I may be forced into a situation where I have to live under the same roof with him, but that doesn't mean I have to go out of my way to converse with him. Honestly, he's lucky I'm speaking to him at all.

"Finn's already gone. I didn't know he left for work so early." His tone is conversational, clearly an attempt to fill the awkward silence.

"I'm guessing there's not much you know anymore." I keep my back to him as I rummage through the pantry for something to eat.

"I guess that's probably true." He pauses. "So, he's working at Jim's shop still."

"Yep. Among other things." I grab a Pop-Tart and quickly close the pantry.

Normally I wouldn't eat something like this for breakfast, because I'm not huge on sweets, other than ice cream. But I'm in such a rush to get out of this kitchen, and it's the easiest, fastest thing I can find.

"The last time we talked he said things were going pretty well for you two. Financially, I mean."

"I didn't realize you two spoke about such things." I grit my teeth.

I know that my brother made it a point to visit Ryland at least once a month, but we never discussed the details of those visits. Truthfully, I never wanted to know. I didn't agree with Finn visiting him. I guess I understood why he did, but I wanted no part in it. To me, Ryland Thorpe is a liar. And I have no time in my life for people I can't trust.

"We talked about a lot of things. He told me about how much you've grown. Although I couldn't picture it. I guess in my head you were still that same little girl who used to follow me around the house begging for piggyback rides."

"Listen." I spin around, my juice in one hand, toaster pastry in the other. "We don't have to do this." I gesture between us.

"Do what?" He quirks an eyebrow at me, acting like he has no idea what I'm talking about, even though I'm pretty damn sure he isn't that dense.

"We aren't friends."

"We were once upon a time." His eyes go down to where his fingers are closed around his coffee cup before they slowly lift to mine again.

"*Were* being the operative word. As in past tense. We don't have to pretend like everything is good. It isn't. I think I made it pretty clear I don't want you here, but for whatever reason, my brother has chosen to ignore my feelings on the matter. He may not hold the choices you made against you, but I do. So, if you'll excuse me." With that, I spin around and quickly exit the kitchen.

I can't keep my head straight at work. I mix up two tables' orders and even manage to spill ranch dressing down some poor woman's blouse after it slid off my tray when I was setting her food down.

It's been one of those days.

"Hey, you okay?" Lily slides up next to me at the food window, where I'm waiting for my last table's order to come up. "You seem off today."

"Off is putting it mildly." I blow out a breath through my nose as I turn toward my best friend.

I'm met with big brown eyes and a head full of black hair.

"What's going on?" She shifts to face me, her forehead creased in concern.

"Ryland's out," I blurt, still not able to fully wrap my head around this fact.

I thought I had more time. More time to prepare. More time to get the hell out of dodge. Just more time.

"Wait, what?" Her eyes go wide. "I thought he still had a couple more years?"

"Apparently, he got out early for good behavior. And the kicker, Finn knew he was being released and never said a word to me."

"Wow." She shakes her head slowly from side to side.

"Oh no, just wait. It gets better." I give her a knowing look. "Finn's letting him stay with us, in Dad's old room."

"Shut the fuck up." She gives me her famous *oh shit* smile.

"Yep. So now, not only is he a free man, but he's also living under the same roof as me."

"Why would Finn let him stay with you guys? Especially since he knows how you feel."

"That's a question I sure would like to know the answer to. It's like Finn never blamed Ryland for anything. The man almost got my brother thrown in jail on drug trafficking charges. You would think he would see that he can't trust him. And yet, he went to visit him regularly and now he's *helping him get back on his feet.*" I put air quotes around the words. "It makes no sense."

"There has to be more to it," Lily interjects.

Of course, this is pure speculation on her part. Lily wasn't around when all of this went down. While she may be my closest friend now, we only met two years ago when we both started working at Milo's Café. We hit it off instantly and have pretty much been inseparable ever since.

"I don't think there is. I think Finn is just that naïve. He thinks because they've been friends their whole lives that Ryland wouldn't do anything to screw him over. But hello, Ryland took him on a drug deal. Apparently nothing says *I've got your back* like dragging you into illegal activity that could land you in jail for *years.*"

"He probably had no idea he was dealing to an undercover cop," she needlessly points out.

"Obviously." I grunt. "But that doesn't make it any better. Had Finn gone down with him, I would have ended up in the care of the state. Did he care? Nope. So why the hell should I give two craps about him?"

"You shouldn't?" She phrases it as a question, like she's not sure. "So," she hesitates, chewing on her bottom lip, "is he still as sexy as he used to be?"

"Lily!" I smack her arm. "Why would you even ask me that?"

"Because, from the way you described him…" She grins.

"I'm done talking to you now." I turn when Davis appears through the kitchen window, sliding two plates under the heat lamp.

"Table twenty-two. Order up," he announces.

"That's me." Lily claps her hands together, quickly grabbing both plates of food. "Listen, I know you don't trust the guy, but maybe try to pretend like he's not there. That's what I would do."

"Easier said than done," I mutter as Lily turns, heading back out into the dining room.

Lily doesn't know Ryland. She has no idea how overwhelming of a presence he has. It's like he takes up all the space in a room the moment he walks into it.

"How long until your shift is up?" Davis asks from behind me. I swivel in his direction, trying to smooth the sour look on my face.

Davis is a sweet guy, but someone I avoid as much as I can. Mainly because he won't stop asking me out, no matter how many times I say no.

"Just waiting on the order for my last table." I square my shoulders.

"I couldn't help but overhear that you're having some issues on the home front. I'd be happy to offer you somewhere to hang if you need to avoid going home for a few hours." He gives me a smile, revealing two matching dimples on each of his freckled cheeks.

Davis is cute, a little short and scrawny for my taste, but still cute. He has the bluest eyes I've ever seen, freckles for days, and a head full of blonde curls. Unfortunately, he's the exact opposite of the guys I'm usually attracted to.

Ryland's face immediately pops into my head but I quickly push it aside. He may be gorgeous, but he's also trouble. The worst kind of trouble. The kind that spends years convincing you that he would do anything to protect you when, in reality, he never cared about you to begin with.

That's the part that hurts most of all. I can pretend like my anger spurs from the fact that he was dealing drugs after he knew my mom left because she was a junkie. I can pretend that it's what he could have done to Finn by bringing him along on a deal. But when it really boils down, I'm most angry with him because I thought I was important to him and it turns out I wasn't. Otherwise he never would have done what he did.

"So, what do you say?" Davis pulls me from my thoughts and I take two slow blinks, trying to remember what we were just talking about. "You wanna hang out after work? Maybe go grab some dinner or something?"

"I appreciate the offer, but I have way too much class work to get done this weekend. Finals are in two weeks and if I want any hope of finishing the semester with my target GPA, I have to buckle down."

"Okay." He seems disappointed but tries to cover it with an easy smile. "Maybe another time."

"Maybe," I agree, my gaze darting to Chet as he slides up next to Davis.

"You have the two chicken salads?" he asks, holding up two large bowls.

"That's me." I nod, reaching over the counter to take the food from him. "Thanks, Chet." I smile at both men before quickly turning and heading back out into the dining room.

Chapter 4

Ryland

"So, how was your first day of freedom?" Finn asks, kicking his shoes off right inside the door.

"Not great. But it sure beats living behind bars any day." I flip off the television.

"Please don't tell me you've spent the entire day inside." He gives me a pointed look. "You've been trapped in a tiny cell for five years. You should be outside, enjoying the amazing weather. You know we're only going to get a few days like this."

He's not wrong. May in Southern Michigan is unpredictable at best. It's freezing ass cold at the beginning of the month. Then there are a few good days in the middle, and by the end you're sweating your balls off.

"I just wanted to hang inside today. Kind of ease my way back into the real world." I lean forward, resting my elbows just above my knees.

"I get that. Any luck on the Ainsley front?"

I know Finn was hoping that Ainsley would see me and all would be forgiven but I knew better. If she had forgiven me on sight, she wouldn't be the same girl I knew. My Ainsley doesn't trust easily. Lose that trust, and you're going to have to work your ass off to earn it back, if you even can.

"Well, she didn't try to physically harm me if that's what you're asking. But she's certainly not happy about me being here."

"Give her time." He plops down on the opposite side of the couch from me. "She'll come around."

"I don't know if she will."

"She will if I tell her..."

"No. You're the person she counts on the most. I can't imagine what it would do to her to find out you've been lying to her. I can take her hating me. You won't be able to take her hating you."

He runs a hand through his dark hair and looks up at the ceiling. "I'm sorry, dude." He lets out a heavy sigh. "This is all my fault. All of it. If I had handled things differently. If I hadn't agreed to…"

"Stop," I cut him off. "We've been through this a hundred times. I made my choice. You have nothing to apologize for. What's done is done. I just want to put the last five years behind me and move the fuck on. Think we can do that?"

He nods, his face strewn with uncertainty and guilt. It's the same way he'd looked at me every time he came to visit me in prison.

"Speaking of moving on," he continues after a long pause. "I talked to Jim today. Turns out Ralph is done at the end of next week. He's going to need someone to take his place. It's nothing fancy. Oil changes, tire rotations, basic shit. But it'll give you a place to start. The pay isn't all that great either but it's better than nothing."

"Wait," I straighten my posture, "are you saying he's willing to give me a job?"

"You start training Monday. If you want it." He nods, his gaze swinging to mine.

"Fuck yeah I want it."

"Well then it's yours."

"What about my felony? He's cool having an ex-con working for him?"

"Fuck, dude, half the guys there are ex-cons. You should feel right at home. Even Jim served time in the nineties for robbing his girlfriend's old man." He chuckles. "I thought you knew that."

"I vaguely remember hearing something about that," I admit. "I can't thank you enough for this, though. Seriously, Finn. Thank you."

He holds a hand up to stop me from saying more.

"I owe you more than I could ever possibly repay you. I don't know what I would have done…"

"Let's not rehash the past. You and Ainsley are my family. I did what I had to do to protect my family."

"Ains will come around," he says again. "Just give her some time."

As if right on cue, the front door swings open and Ainsley walks inside, her cell phone pressed to her ear with one hand as she balances two takeout containers in the other.

I still can't wrap my head around how much she's changed these last five years.

Ainsley Kenter has always been beautiful. With long dark hair and bright green eyes, she's the kind of girl that always had everyone, guy and girl alike, eating out of the palm of her hand. But gone is the cute girl I once considered my little sister. Replaced by a young woman so fucking beautiful I can barely tear my eyes off her as she walks into the room.

When I saw her last night for the first time in half a decade, I was pretty certain that I forgot how to fucking speak. And it has nothing to do with the fact that I've been incarcerated for the past five years and two months, but everything to do with the fact that she's just that stunning.

Seeing her all grown up is bittersweet. It's incredible to see the amazing young woman she's become but it hurts to know that I wasn't here to see it all happen.

I was here the day they brought her home from the hospital. I was here for every milestone, every birthday, every special occasion, and even the not so special ones. I was here through it all, until I wasn't.

Knowing I missed so much, seeing the disdain on her face when she looks at me now, it's like taking a knife to the fucking gut. The girl who once looked at me like I was her world, now looks at me like she sees right through me.

"Hey, Ains," Finn calls over his shoulder as she uses her foot to kick the door shut.

"Hey." She doesn't look in my direction. "I brought you some stuff from the restaurant. You can have whatever you want. I already ate." She leans over the back of the couch, setting the two containers on the cushion next to him.

"Thanks. You got any plans tonight?" he asks, his gaze following her as she steps to the end of the couch, pausing directly behind me.

I don't look over my shoulder, no matter how badly I want to.

"I have some schoolwork to finish up so don't be surprised if you don't see me for the rest of the weekend. I plan on locking myself in my room until all of it is done."

"Well, make sure you at least come out to eat, yeah?" He smiles at her.

"I make no promises." I hear the laughter in her voice, followed by footsteps as she continues on to her room.

"That girl." Finn shakes his head. "You hungry?" He gestures to the food containers sitting between us. "Knowing Ains, she brought home cheese sticks, fried pickles, and nachos." He chuckles. "I swear she's trying to fatten me up." He picks up the top container and passes it to me. I don't have much of an appetite but I take it anyway.

I open it, revealing a mountain of nachos smothered in meat, jalapenos, and cheese sauce, among other things. My mouth instantly waters. They definitely don't have food like this at Rockwood Penitentiary.

"Told ya." Finn laughs when he opens the other container and finds cheese sticks and fried pickles. "So predictable."

"Maybe she's got a point." I gesture toward him. "You are looking a little thin." I pick up a nacho overflowing with toppings and shovel it into my mouth, practically moaning around the bite.

"Thin?" He flexes a bicep. "It's called lean muscle."

"Is that what it's called?" I chuckle around my mouthful of food.

"Fuck you. It's not like we all have had countless hours to spend working out." He throws me a side eye.

"You got me. I wanted to go to jail for that very reason," I deadpan.

"Shut up." He chomps down on a cheese stick, the cheese oozing out, causing him to have to stuff the whole thing into his mouth to avoid wearing half of it. "At least you made the best of it," he adds once he's swallowed his food. "You're more ripped than you've ever been before."

"Well, like you said. I had a lot of free time." I shrug, shoveling another nacho into my mouth.

We spend the next hour lounging around the living room, bullshitting about nothing of real significance. Honestly, it feels good to be here again. In some ways it feels like I never left.

The floor still has the same worn and chipped hardwood. The walls are still painted the same gray and need some serious touch ups. The same furniture still sits in the exact same spots. It's like I left for five years and not one thing changed. Well, with the house anyway.

Other things have changed in ways I never imagined they would.

I knew when Ainsley never came to see me in jail that she was mad at me. And while I didn't want her to visit me because I didn't want her to ever step foot in a place like that, it still stung a little. I expected that sting to lessen as time went on but that wasn't the case. The older she got, and the more time that had passed, the worse it was for me.

I hated the thought of everything I was missing. I told myself over and over again, if I could just see her, explain things to her, then I could make her understand. But she never came and I never got the chance.

Not that I would have ever told her the truth. I wouldn't do that to Finn. But I needed to somehow make her see that everything I did, I did for her.

Now, I'm afraid it's too little too late. We aren't the same people we were five years ago. And no matter how much I want to force things between us to be okay, I know I have to let it happen with time.

I just hope one day she can see that I'm still the same guy I've always been. The one who was like a second brother to her for all those years. The one she used to look at as part of her family.

Because now she doesn't look at me like that anymore. Hell, she barely looks at me at all. The thought is a sobering one, and has me slipping off to my bedroom before eight o'clock in an effort to try to sleep off the reminders this day brought back.

I knew coming here after being away for so long would be difficult, I just didn't realize it would be to this degree. What once felt like home, feels more like the prison cell I just got out of.

I hate to think of it that way but I also can't help it. In some strange way, being shut in this bedroom feels like being locked away all over again, especially when the person I want to talk to the most won't look at me.

I plop back on the bed, not bothering to turn on any lights. The sun has almost completely set, casting a low orange glow into the room that fits my mood.

Tucking my hands behind my head, I look up at the ceiling, trying to sort through the array of emotions that have swarmed me since I stepped into this house yesterday. And that's when I hear her voice.

Ainsley.

She must be on the phone. She's obviously not used to having someone in the room next to her so she probably hasn't considered that I can hear her through the paper-thin walls.

"I don't know, Lily." I can hear the uncertainty in her voice. For some reason, it makes me more curious as to what they're talking about.

I know I shouldn't be listening to their conversation. What twenty-six-year-old man eavesdrops on his best friend's little sister? But I can't seem to help myself. I inch closer to the headboard that sits against the adjoining wall of our bedrooms.

"Nick Porter, though. He's a little old for me, isn't he?" She pauses, presumably listening to the person on the other line. Lily, I think she said. Though that name doesn't sound familiar to me.

There was a point in time when I knew every single person in Ainsley's life. Safe to say that's no longer the case.

"Yeah, but six years isn't as bad. Eleven years is just too big of a gap. Besides, isn't he in the middle of a divorce?" My ears instantly perk up.

Another long pause.

"That was a long time ago though, Lil. I was just a kid."

More silence.

"Yes it makes a difference."

Another pause.

"Yes, okay. He's even sexier now than he was back then, but that's not the point." A brief hesitation. "Lil, would you stop? Just because I was secretly in love with him when I was younger does *not* mean I'm still harboring those feelings.

You know how I feel about him now, probably better than most."

My shoulders go rigid and I swear I can feel my pulse everywhere, thumping through my body like a steady drum.

Is she talking about me?

No.

I quickly shake off the thought. There's no way. Yes, she did used to follow me around like a lost puppy, but she never gave me any indication that she had any sort of crush on me. She was fifteen when I went to jail. If she was harboring feelings for me, I think I would have noticed. Teenage girls aren't the most subtle creatures in the world.

Then again, maybe I never noticed because I was never looking.

Even at fifteen, Ainsley was eye catching. The older she got, the harder it was to continue looking at her like she was my little sister. Every day her beauty grew and every day it became harder not to notice.

I think back to the weeks leading up to my arrest. The way Ainsley would look at me. The things she would say. How weird she had been acting around me.

Maybe it was in front of me all along and I didn't want to see it.

"Okay, I'm done talking to you now. I should have known this is why you called." She laughs and the sound instantly takes me back.

Back to when we would sit up in our favorite tree and talk for hours. Back to long summer days that her, Finn, and I would spend on the lake. Back to a simpler time when she looked at me like I mattered, which is completely different than how she looks at me now.

"No, you cannot come over and see him." Another laugh. "I'm serious, Lil. If you show up here I will not answer the door."

A brief moment of silence passes.

"I already told you no. I have too much schoolwork to get done. Lily." Her tone is playfully threatening. "That bitch just hung up on me," she says presumably to herself, soft music kicking on moments later.

I spend the next several minutes dissecting everything I overheard. Either Ainsley had a thing for me when she was younger, or it just so happens that there's another guy who was in her life back then that just came back into the picture. *Not likely.*

I'm not sure how this news makes me feel. On one hand, I'm uneasy and a little embarrassed that I never noticed. On the other, the thought kind of excites me, which makes me feel incredibly guilty.

Though I'm not sure why it matters now. She's made it pretty clear she wants nothing to do with me anymore.

It's right after nine when I hear a knock on the front door. The music coming from Ainsley's room immediately stops and I hear her bedroom door open moments later. "Fucking, Lily," she grumbles as she stomps down the hall.

Pushing up on my elbows, I try to stop myself from going out there to investigate, but my curiosity is too much to resist. I have to meet this Lily character. Her reaction to me will say a lot about what Ainsley has or hasn't told her.

Not that I even know why I care.

Rolling out of bed, I cross the room, not bothering to put on a shirt before stepping out into the hallway with only a pair of old gym shorts hanging loosely on my hips.

I enter the living room to see Ainsley and another girl, with light brown skin and black hair, talking quietly in the open doorway.

Lily sees me first, her eyes darting over Ainsley's shoulder before widening slightly. I offer her a smile and nod as I turn, veering toward the back of the house.

Less than a minute passes before I sense someone enter the kitchen. Keeping my back to the doorway, I pretend not to notice as I busy myself making a peanut butter and jelly sandwich.

Even though I just ate that entire thing of nachos less than two hours ago, I'm hungry again, so really I'm killing two birds with one stone right now.

"You must be Ryland," an unfamiliar female voice says.

"I am." I slap a second piece of bread on top of my sandwich and turn, taking a large bite as I do.

My eyes land on a girl who I would guess to be about the same age as Ainsley. Her dark hair falls right below her shoulders and she has cute, mousy features that make her look younger than she probably is. Average height. Curvy build. She's a good-looking girl, but definitely no Ainsley.

I don't know where the thought comes from. But it hits me so unexpectantly that I nearly choke on the peanut butter and bread as I try to swallow.

It's one thing to acknowledge she's attractive. It's another to start comparing other women to her.

"Hey, Lil, will you grab me a water while you're in there?" Ainsley calls from the living room.

Women.

I have to resist the urge to chuckle at their lame attempt to cover up what clearly is going on here.

"Yeah," she calls back, her big brown eyes locked on me. "I'm Lily, by the way." She smiles, setting off toward the refrigerator. She pulls it open, grabs two bottles of water, and closes the door, turning to where I'm standing a couple short feet away.

I don't miss the way her gaze dips to my bare torso before coming back up to my face. I'd be lying if I said her reaction didn't give me a little bit of satisfaction. It's been a long time since I've had a woman's eyes on my body.

I really need to get laid.

The thought makes me feel more like myself than I have in a while. That must be it. My unease. My uncertainty. The fact that I've thought about nothing but Ainsley since the moment I stepped in that front door twenty-four hours ago.

I just need to get laid, let off some steam, and remember what it feels like to be Ryland Thorpe again.

"It's nice to meet you, Lily." I nod, tearing off another bite of my sandwich.

"I'm Ainsley's friend. I just came over to help her study."

"That's very nice of you." I pretend to buy the lie.

"Anyways." She slowly starts to back away, her eyes making another sweep of my body as she does. "It was nice to meet you, finally. I've heard a lot about you."

"You have?" I question, finding the statement odd. Considering Ainsley has made it clear she wants nothing to do with me, I find it hard to believe she would say anything about me at all. She seems pretty content pretending that I don't exist.

And yet, I overheard her talking about me tonight. Then again, I only caught the last part of the conversation. Who knows what was said before I started listening.

"Oh yeah. Ainsley talks about you all the time. I swear every memory she has involves you. I especially loved the lake story. Did you really pay her twenty dollars to jump into the water in the middle of December?"

My lips quirk up into a smile.

"Lily, come on!" Ainsley hollers, the irritation in her voice is unmistakable.

"Yeah, well, um, I gotta go," Lily stutters out before quickly turning and disappearing from the kitchen.

I stand there, partially stunned for a long moment. Here I had assumed Ainsley hated me. Maybe she doesn't hate me at all. Maybe she just wants me to think she hates me.

Regardless, I need to get the hell out of this house. I think my biggest problem is that I've been cooped up for far too long. I need to get out of here, have a few beers, and hopefully sink my dick into someone for the first time in five years.

And I know just the place to go...

Chapter 5

Ainsley

"What the hell are you doing?" I hiss at Lily when she comes skipping into the living room, a wide grin on her face. She passes me a bottle of water before twisting the cap off of hers.

"He is gorgeous," she mouths, fanning herself.

As if I didn't already know that...

"You could not have been more obvious," I whisper yell at my best friend.

"Oh stop. He's completely clueless. I played it off well."

I roll my eyes.

"Come on." I grab her arm and drag her down the hallway before shoving her into my bedroom.

"You need to get over your issues with that man and tag him now," she says the instant the door closes. "He is F.I.N.E. Fine, fine, fine."

"Do you need a cold shower?" I give her a pointed look. "He's just a guy and you're over here acting like a dog in heat." I'd be annoyed by her behavior if she wasn't so damn comical.

"I'm not even sure a cold shower would do it." She laughs. "But I think I finally get it. Why you've been so gaga over him for so long. Why you were so pissed when he left. It's all making a lot more sense now."

"Me being pissed at him has nothing to do with him leaving and everything to do with *why* he left."

"Uh huh." She doesn't seem convinced. "Girl, I didn't even know you when he was around but I knew the first moment you said his name that you were in love with him. Then today at work, I could tell you were more flustered by the thought of him being back than you were angry by the fact that he was."

"That's not true. Have you not been listening to anything I've said to you over the past two years?"

"Oh, I heard you alright. I heard you talk incessantly about a man you claimed to hate. I hate to break it to you, Ains, but if you hate someone that much, the last thing you want to do is spend your days talking about them."

"I thought that's what friends are for. To vent to when you're upset about something."

"They are. But let's be real here for a moment. The man went to jail for dealing drugs. It's not like he murdered someone. And yet that's how you're acting."

"It wasn't just that he was dealing drugs, it was that he put Finn in danger."

"Even still. Clearly Finn has forgiven him. Which begs the question, why can't you?"

"Whose side are you on?" I fire off, my quick temper getting the better of me.

"Yours. Of course." She seems offended by my question. "I can't even believe you would ask me that."

"Well, when you're standing here advocating for the enemy."

"I'm not advocating for anyone. I get your issues with him. I'd be pissed too if the shoe was on the other foot. All I'm saying is do you really think what he did is *that* unforgivable or are you holding onto your anger for another reason?"

"What other reason would there be?"

"Do you really want me to say?" She gives me a knowing look.

"No," I reply flatly, having a pretty good idea what she's going to say.

But she's wrong… Isn't she?

I shake off the thought.

"Listen, I have tons of work to get done. So unless you're actually planning on helping me study, you can go now." I turn, flopping down on my bed that has several textbooks and notepads spread across it.

"Is that anyway to talk to your best friend?"

"Considering you came over after I specifically told you not to, then made a spectacle of checking out a man I can't stand, *yes*, that's exactly how I'm going to talk to you."

She studies me for a long moment before her features soften.

"You're right. I'm sorry. I was just so damn curious. I've heard you talk about him a gazillion times. How could I not be at least a little intrigued?"

"I think gazillion is a bit of an overstatement."

"Okay, fine. A million. Is that better?"

"Not really, no." A small laugh escapes my lips.

"Oh shut up." She waves a hand at me as she crosses to the other side of my bed, plopping down next to me moments later. "So, what are we working on?"

"Right now I'm trying to study for my Political Science final."

"Well, I will be zero help there. How about I sit on my phone and offer emotional support?" she offers, grinning as she leans forward to pull her cell phone out of the back pocket of her jeans.

"Emotional support." I shake my head at her. "Fine," I concede. "But if you so much as utter *his* name even once for the remainder of the evening, I reserve the right to hit you with this." I hold up an extremely thick book.

"You have my word." She laughs, tracing an X over her heart with the tip of her pointer finger.

Laughing, I position myself with my back against the headboard and flip back to the chapter I was reviewing before Lily showed up, hoping like hell I can concentrate enough to retain even a fraction of the information.

It's after eleven when Lily decides to head home for the night. It isn't until after she's gone and I'm getting ready to go back into my room that I notice Ryland's door is open.

Taking a step back, I peer inside. The room is dark and from what I can tell, empty. Curious, I head further down the hall to Finn's room. His door is also open and his room is empty.

It's not like Finn to leave without telling me first, so I assume they must be here somewhere. Then again, neither of them were in the living room or the kitchen, so I'm really not sure where they could be.

Heading back to my room, I snag my cell phone off my dresser and pull up Finn's name, hitting the call button. It rings twice before he picks up.

"Hey, Ains. Everything okay?" His voice is distorted by the amount of background noise filtering into the speaker of the phone.

"Yeah, fine. I just wasn't sure where you went."

"Sorry, I knew you were studying and I didn't want to bother you. I'm actually down at Moe's having a few drinks with Ryland."

"Oh, okay."

"Lily still there?"

"No, she just left."

"Well, we won't be gone much longer. Though given the way Regina Tinsley is acting right now, I wouldn't be surprised if only one of us returns home this evening." I know immediately that he's referring to the town slut. I don't even run in that crowd but I know all about her.

My stomach twists uncomfortably.

"Is Ryland allowed to stay out overnight?" I feel stupid asking the question.

"He's on probation, Ains. Not house arrest." He chuckles, clearly inebriated.

"Gotcha. Well, just do me a favor and be safe."

Even though Moe's is only a couple of blocks from here, I hate the idea of him walking home at night, especially after drinking. Finn may be an able-bodied man, but we don't live in the best neighborhood.

"Always am. Call if you need anything."

"Will do." I hang up the phone, the knot in my stomach growing tighter.

I try to push past the feeling as I kill the lights and climb into bed, throwing the thick comforter over my head, but it proves impossible to do.

Every time I close my eyes all I can see is Regina with Ryland. Her lips, that she always has painted a bright shade of red, on his. Her fake nails raking up his back. Her name on his lips. And while thinking about Ryland with another girl has always bothered me, it's never felt quite this overwhelming.

I toss and turn for the next hour, unable to shut my brain off.

I wake when I hear someone come in the front door right after one. I quickly clamor out of bed and head for the hallway. I pull open my bedroom door, expecting to see my brother. Instead, who I see sends my heart knocking into my ribs with the force of a sledgehammer.

"Ryland," I sputter, coming to an abrupt halt in my doorway. "Where's Finn?" I stick my head out into the hall and look both ways, not seeing my brother anywhere.

"He went home with Regina." He gives me a funny look like he thought I already knew.

"Oh." I don't try to hide my surprise. "I thought…"

"You thought *I* was going home with Regina." He steals the words right from my mouth.

"I just assumed." My voice shakes slightly. "I mean, you *have* been in prison for five years." As if that's some type of justification. "I'm sure you have… needs." My face heats but for some reason I can't stop the word vomit from continuing to spew from my mouth. "I wouldn't blame you if you needed to…" I bite my bottom lip in an attempt to silence myself.

"Truthfully, that's why I went out tonight," he admits, taking a step toward me. "But when I got there I realized that none of the women there were who I wanted." His eyes dip to my mouth before coming back up to my eyes. There's an intensity behind his stare that I don't think I've ever seen before.

It's enough to send my already frazzled nerves spiraling out of control. And I have no idea who he's even talking about. But I want to pretend it's me. I want to pretend that I'm the woman he wants.

I want to grab the collar of his shirt and pull him into my room. Kiss him the way I've dreamt about kissing him for most of my life.

Make love to him the way I have done a million times in my dreams. But then I remember that this isn't the Ryland Thorpe I once *thought* I knew so well.

That man doesn't exist. The one in front of me is nothing more than a liar.

This seems to snap me from the fog threatening to swallow me whole. I blink once, slowly, and then take a full step back.

"Well, have a good night." I plaster on the best smile I can muster before quickly closing the door between us.

Chapter 6

Ainsley

Six years ago

"Ryland, stop." I squirm, trying to break free of his grasp. He squeezes my side again, causing me to squeal in laughter.

He knows how much I hate being tickled.

Rearing back, I elbow him in the center of his stomach. He lets out a whoosh of air and his hold on me falters. Using this as my way out, I twist and manage to duck under his arm before he has time to stop me.

Breaking free, I take off running down the beach. It's dark so I can barely see a thing. But I can hear. Which means I know Ryland is getting close.

Seconds later, an arm snakes around my stomach and I'm hauled against a hard body.

"And just where do you think you're going?" Laughter is in his voice.

"Away from you." I lift my feet up and Ryland easily supports my weight.

"Your brother would kill me if he knew I let you talk me into this. Are you trying to get us

both in trouble?" His breath is hot on the side of my face.

"How would I do that?" I lower my feet and Ryland releases me.

"I don't know, maybe if you get hurt sprinting in the dark. You can't see anything. What if you fell and broke a bone or something?"

I snort, spinning around to face him.

"I can see you just fine." His gorgeous face is illuminated under the light of the full moon.

"Yeah, only because I'm standing right in front of you," he argues.

"I think you're afraid of being left alone in the dark," I tease.

"Or maybe I'm afraid of you being alone in the dark. Pretty little thing like you. A town like this." He shakes his head, his expression growing serious.

He says something else, but truthfully I stopped listening to him after he called me pretty. *Because of this, I'm not sure how to respond when he stops talking.*

In an effort to cover up this fact, I reach down and grip the hem of my sundress, quickly pulling it up and over my head before depositing it into the sand.

Ryland's eyes stay on my face. They always stay on my face. Just once I wish he would look at me. Really look at me. That he would see me for more than just Finn's little sister. And while my bathing suit is very modest, it doesn't hide the evidence that I'm not a little girl anymore. I just wish he could acknowledge that.

"You really want to do this?" He arches a brow at me. "It's only been warm a couple of weeks. The water is probably freezing cold."

"I'm sure. I've swam in colder." I smile, giving him a knowing look.

"Okay, just remember that this was your idea." He takes off his shirt, and even though I know I shouldn't, I take a brief moment to look at him.

He's so beautiful.

"Ains?" He must sense where my focus is, because when I look back up, he's got a weird look on his face.

"Last one into the water has to buy the other a soda," I announce, nearly falling flat on my face when I turn and make a move for the water.

Ryland laughs, zooming past me before I have a chance to right myself. He beats me to the water with no problem at all, but he doesn't stay there long.

He no more than dives in before he's running back out, his arms wrapped around his torso.

"You're such a baby," I call as he passes me right as I enter the lake.

I run in until the water hits my knees and then I dive headfirst. It's so cold that for a brief moment all my joints lock up and I'm not sure I can move. And while yes, I've swam in colder water, that was for only thirty seconds and by the time I got out I was pretty certain I was going to die of hypothermia. A bit dramatic I know, but I had never felt pain like that before. It was like being stabbed with a thousand tiny needles all over my body and for the life of me, I could not get warm.

This water isn't as bad, but it still catches me a bit off guard. I push up to the surface, sucking in a deep breath of air.

Even though I don't want to give Ryland the satisfaction of being right, I know there is no way I'm going to last more than a minute in this frigid water.

I immediately turn and start heading back toward the shore, my teeth chattering the entire way.

Ryland is standing at the edge of the water. The smile on his face is evident from several feet away.

"Told you it was too cold." He chuckles, handing me my sundress the moment I reach him. "And you owe me a soda." He waits until I'm

dressed before tugging me against his chest. Wrapping his arms around me, he rubs his hands vigorously up and down my arms in an effort to warm me.

While the water was ice cold, I'd jump in it all over again for this.

Resting my head on his chest, I breathe in his scent. A mixture of his own unique smell, deodorant, and lake water. The smell is intoxicating and all I want to do is stay right here for the rest of my life.

"Come on." Ryland breaks the moment all too soon. He turns, keeping one arm wrapped around my shoulders as he leads me back up the beach. "We should probably get to the truck before one or both of us catches pneumonia."

"I had no idea the water would be that cold."

"Pretty sure I tried to tell you it would be."

"Pretty sure no one likes an I told you so," I fire back.

He shakes his head, laughter rolling through his body as he squeezes me tighter against his side.

"If you tell Finn about this, I'm going to deny, deny, deny." He stops at the passenger side of his beat up, old Ford truck.

"Shut up. You're going to end up telling him the moment we walk into the house and you

know it." I *smack playfully at his chest, turning to climb into the truck when he tugs open the door.*

"You know me so well." He *grins, winking at me before slamming the door closed.*

Chapter 7

Ainsley

"Can you believe Professor Lumbar?" Matt slides up next to me as we exit our English Lit class. "Like we don't have enough on our plates right now?" He groans.

He's referring to that fact that our teacher just dropped a bomb on us that our final assignment for his class is a five-thousand-word essay on the way classic literature has impacted modern literature. As if that wasn't a difficult enough subject to write about, especially for me, a sociology major, we only have until next week to complete it.

"I will be so glad when this class is over," I agree. Professor Lumbar is one of the most challenging professors I've had in my two years at Wayne State University. "I have to take one more English class during summer semester and I'm really hoping he's not my only option."

"I can't believe you're enrolling for summer classes… *Again*." He follows me out of the building into the warm afternoon.

"Summer courses are a must if I hope to graduate next May. Why drag it out if I don't have to?"

"Well, I for one, rather enjoy my summer breaks."

"That's because your family owns a lake house in Tennessee. I'd probably take my summers off too if it meant I could lay out lakeside all summer drinking beer and getting tan."

I think it's safe to say Matt and I come from very different worlds. He grew up about an hour north of here in an upper-class suburb and now has his own apartment not far from campus that he shares with two other students. I grew up, and still live, on the outskirts of Detroit in what most people would probably refer to as the ghetto.

He convinced me to go on a date with him once last year. When he took me to some fancy Italian restaurant with a dress code, I figured that maybe we weren't very compatible. But despite what was probably the worst first date in history, we've remained friends, and pretty good ones at that.

"It's not like I spend the entire summer there. I usually only go down for a couple of weeks. You could always come with me. I already told you my parents would love to have you." He smiles at me.

"I appreciate the offer but you know I can't." I adjust the strap of my book bag across my shoulder as I head toward the parking lot.

"One of these days I'm going to get you to loosen up a little and have some fun." He knocks his shoulder into mine, but because of our height difference he has to bend down to do it.

"I know how to have fun," I argue, throwing him a sideways glance.

Matt is what I would call a *pretty boy*. Tall. Athletic. Blond hair. Blue eyes. Perfect sun kissed skin, even though we live in Michigan which has more cold days than warm ones. And while I'm perfectly aware of how attractive he is, I've never really felt a spark between the two of us.

"Sure you do," he says sarcastically. "I guess if your definition of fun is work, school, work, school, then yes, you're a natural born party animal."

"We can't all live the charmed life."

"I wouldn't say my life is charmed, but it sure as hell is a lot more interesting than yours," he teases.

"On that note." I stop next to my car. "I guess I'll see you Thursday?" I ask as Matt continues on toward his SUV, two spaces over.

Our cars are another perfect example of the differences between our worlds. Mine is an old Malibu that's been on its last leg for months. His is a brand-new Subaru that his parents bought for him.

Some people get all the luck.

"Yep, see you then," he calls back, disappearing inside the shiny vehicle moments later.

I let out a heavy breath and pull my door open, cringing when it scrapes and squeals like it's about to fall off the hinges. Tossing my book bag into the passenger seat, I slide behind the steering wheel and close the door.

I've just jammed the key into the ignition when a knock on my window startles me. I jump and glance to the side, Matt's straight, too white teeth the first thing I see.

"Jeez," I mutter, trying to calm my sudden rapid heartbeat as I roll down the window. "Are you trying to give me a heart attack?"

"Sorry." He chuckles. "I just realized I have nothing to do for the rest of the day. Do you wanna hit up Chelsea's for ice cream and catch an afternoon movie?"

The invite is tempting. It's not every day that I have an afternoon off work, and it is only one-thirty. But I also know I need to get a head start on this English paper if I want any hopes of finishing it on time.

At the same time, the thought of going home is not something that sits well with me, either. After the weekend I had, it's the last place I want to be.

I successfully avoided Ryland the entire day Sunday, but I doubt I'll be able to keep it up for long. It's not like I can just live in my bedroom. Then again, that's where I've always spent the majority of my time.

I go back and forth for a few seconds before finally deciding that I could use some time out with a friend.

"You know what, that actually sounds perfect." I smile, pulling the keys out of the ignition. I'm sure Matt will want to drive. Not that I can blame him. If I had his car I wouldn't want to ride in mine either.

Grabbing cash and my cell out of the front pocket of my book bag, I roll the window back up before shoving the door open and climbing out.

"Would you mind swinging me by Jim's Auto Repair on our way? I need to drop some money off to Finn. I got paid this morning and I'd rather give it to him so he can stop at the bank after work," I ask, sliding the small stack of bills into my front pocket.

"Yep, we can do that." He nods, following me to his SUV.

"Also, you're going to need to feed me lunch before you stuff me full of ice cream." I smile when he pulls the passenger door open for me.

"So demanding." He huffs playfully, waiting until I'm settled in my seat before closing the door.

"What can I say, I need sustenance," I jest once he's sitting in the driver's seat next to me.

"Any place in particular?" he asks, firing the engine to life.

"Nah, just surprise me."

"You got it." He winks, popping the car into drive.

"Do you want me to go in with you?" Matt asks, backing into a parking spot outside of Jim's.

The shop is packed today, with a line of cars wrapping around the entire garage waiting to be serviced.

"Yeah, if you don't mind. I hate going in there by myself." Not that the guys at the shop are bad people or anything, but some of them have wandering eyes that make me feel a little uncomfortable anytime I have to walk through the garage.

"Not a problem." He kills the engine and follows me out of the car.

"This shouldn't take but a second."

"We're not in any rush." He shrugs casually, pulling open the glass door that leads into the lobby for me.

Tellers, Jim's teenage nephew, is working the front desk, per usual. After getting into several fights at school, his mom decided to home school him for his last year of high school, which equates to him working the front desk at her brother's shop while he 'attends' school online.

He offers me a simple nod as we enter.

"Finn in the back?" I ask, getting another nod before his eyes go back to the computer in front of him.

"He's talkative," Matt grumbles behind me as we make our way into the large, and rather noisy garage.

"He's a troubled kid. I feel bad for him," I say, veering off toward the far-right station of the garage where Finn usually works.

The shop isn't Finn's only job, but it's his longest running employment and the one that offers the most hours each week. Therefore also brings in the brunt of his income. In addition to working here, he also does some roofing work with a buddy and bartends at Moe's on an on-call basis.

When I spot the lower half of someone sticking out from underneath the hood of a supped-up Mustang, I hold my finger up to my lips to make sure Matt stays quiet before tip toeing around the car.

"What are you doing?" I yell, causing Finn to jump and knock his head on the underside of the hood.

"What the hell, Ains?" he grumbles, emerging from under the hood, rubbing the back of his head.

"Sorry." I laugh. "I couldn't help myself."

He shakes his head at me before his eyes move to Matt.

"You remember Matt from school, right?" I ask, my gaze sliding to the guy standing next to me.

"Yep." Finn nods. "How's it going, Matt?" he asks, tossing a grease covered rag over his shoulder.

"It's going well. Ainsley and I were just about to grab lunch and catch a movie."

"Sounds like fun." His attention comes back to me. "Did you need some money or something?" he asks, clearly not remembering that today is Monday, which is when I typically bring *him* money after the restaurant cashes out our checks for us.

It's not much, considering I make less than five dollars an hour, but it's my contribution toward the bills. My tips are where I make the most money, and that gets used for school expenses, gas, food, and any extras I need.

"When was the last time I asked you for money?" I give him a knowing look. I may not make much but I make enough to pay for my own stuff. "I wanted to give *you* money so I'm not walking around with it in my pocket." I dig the bills out of my jeans and extend them to him. "It's only one–twenty, but it should cover the electric bill if you want to stop and deposit it on your way home."

"Oh shit. I forgot it's Monday." He snags his wallet out of his back pocket before shoving the bills inside.

"Hey, Finn, what was that part number again?" I turn to see Ryland round the other side of the car. "I can't find it so I'm thinking I either wrote the wrong number down or we're out and are going to have to order it." He looks up from the piece of paper in his hand, freezing when he catches sight of me.

He looks temporarily caught off guard but quickly regains his composure as he offers me a small nod before his eyes go to Matt.

He stares at him for a long moment before Finn's voice pulls him back to the matter at hand.

"C7849," Finn rambles off the part number by memory. It's no wonder he remembers this stuff. He's been working here since high school.

"Okay." Ryland glances down at the paper. "Yeah, we're going to have to order this part. You want me to call the owner and let him know it's going to be a couple of days?"

"Yeah." Finn steps back from the car and shuts the hood. "Just tell him we'll give him ten percent off for the wait."

"Will do." Ryland nods, quickly spinning around and heading back in the direction of the office without looking in my direction again.

"Since when does he work here?" I wait until he's out of earshot to ask.

"Since today." Finn grabs the rag off his shoulder and wipes his hands.

"Let me guess, you got him the job?" I cross my arms over my chest.

"I did." He squares his shoulders. "You need to stop giving him such a hard time. The man has spent the last five years in prison. Cut him a little slack."

"Why should I? He made his own bed. Now he can lie in it," I clip.

"I'm serious, Ainsley. I understand you're angry but you need to start letting this go. For everyone's sake. He did what he did. It's over now. He's not going anywhere and neither are you, so you need to find a way to deal with him being back."

"I don't..." I start, but Finn holds up a hand, cutting me off.

"I'm not discussing this here." His eyes dart behind me and only then do I realize that a couple of the other guys are working on a car not too far from us and can likely hear every word. "Just think about what I said."

"Fine," I grumble, turning to Matt. "Are you about ready to get out of here?"

"Whenever you are." He nods.

"I guess I'll see you at home later," I tell Finn, spinning toward the exit.

"Okay. You two have fun."

"We will," I holler over my shoulder, making a beeline for the door.

When Ryland steps out of the office as we're approaching, I loop my arm through Matt's and tug him closer. Matt, who clearly has no idea what I'm doing, throws a lifted eyebrow in my direction.

I give him a wide smile and a look that says *play along*, before turning my attention forward.

I have no idea what I'm trying to accomplish by flaunting Matt in front of Ryland, but I do it anyway. Maybe in some way I'm hoping to get a reaction out of him, although I'm not entirely sure why. If I despise him as much as I tell everyone I do, why the hell do I care what he thinks about me walking arm in arm with another guy?

"Ainsley," Ryland says my name as we pass.

"Ryland," I return, not missing the way his jaw clenches when his gaze goes to Matt.

My inner cheerleader does a backflip.

No matter how much I try to pretend I hate Ryland, deep down I know I could never hate him. I can hate what he did. I can hate that he left. But I can't hate him.

Because somewhere, buried deep, there still lives a piece of the girl I used to be. A girl who gave her heart to a man who didn't even know he had it. And that girl, she still loves Ryland Thorpe. Honestly, I think maybe she always will.

I can feel Ryland's eyes on us long after we've passed and I have to physically restrain myself from turning around to prove myself right.

"Who was that?" Matt gives me a questioning look as we hit the parking lot and head toward his car.

"Who?" I play stupid, even though I know *he's* not stupid.

"Really, Ainsley? You couldn't have been more obvious if you had tried." He releases my arm seconds before opening my door for me.

Always the gentleman. "The guy you were clearly trying to make jealous."

"I wasn't trying to make him jealous."

"Sure you weren't." He chuckles. "I may not be the quickest person in the world, but even I picked up on the weird tension between you two. From what you were saying to Finn, I got the impression you don't care for him. But if that's the case, why parade me through the garage like a trophy?"

"I was *not* parading you. I was just trying to make a point. And I don't care for him. He just got out of jail and is staying with us and I'm not very happy about it." I snap my seat belt into place, trying to appear completely natural even though I feel like anything but.

Every interaction with Ryland rattles me. It always has.

"You're sure that's it?" He studies me for a long moment.

"I'm sure. Now can we go already? I'm starving." I rub my stomach dramatically.

Matt doesn't look completely convinced but he decides not to push the issue further. It's not like we're the kind of friends that tell each other everything. We're more of the casual, hang out when it's convenient, type of friends. And those types of friends I do not share things as intricate and fragile as my relationship with Ryland Thorpe.

"Have you decided what you're in the mood for?" he asks a few moments later as he settles into the driver's seat.

"I already told ya, surprise me."

"You say that, but the last time I tried to surprise you, you didn't seem too impressed."

"That's because you took me to a restaurant so upscale I *had* to wear a dress. But you know me a lot better now, and you know what I would probably like and what I wouldn't. So, you pick. And make it good."

"Gahhh, it's too much pressure." He laughs.

"Tell you what. Name three types of food that sound good and I'll pick the one that sounds the best. That should at least help you narrow it down."

"I like that idea." He starts the car. "Chinese, pizza, or subs," he quickly rambles off.

"Hmmm. That's a tough one." I tap my chin. "On one hand, I love Chinese food. But, pizza is usually my go to. Then again, I wouldn't hate a sub right now."

"Oh my god, woman, just pick already." Laughter rumbles through his voice.

"Subs," I announce.

"You're sure?"

"I'm sure. Considering most sub restaurants are on the same caliber, I think it's the one choice you're least likely to screw up," I tease.

"You're probably right." He chuckles, popping the car into gear before slowly pulling out of the parking spot.

I'm giggling over our conversation when I catch sight of Ryland standing in the lobby, his gaze trained on me and Matt as we pull away.

I can't help but look back as we pull out onto the street, but I lose sight of him too quickly to really gauge his expression. Considering the lobby of the shop is floor to ceiling windows, I have no doubt that he could see us from where he was standing. The only real question is, was he watching us and if so, why?

It's a question that nags at me through lunch and ice cream, and is still weighing on my mind as we settle into the movie theater.

My mind drifts back to Saturday night. The way Ryland looked at me. How his eyes darkened when they dropped to my lips. If I didn't know any better, I'd say he wanted to kiss me as badly as I wanted him to. And yet, for reasons I'm not sure I entirely understand, I shut the door in his face.

I've waited my entire life to have Ryland look at me that way and yet as he stood there, every single warning bell was blaring in my head.

Because no matter how badly a part of me still wants him, I know that I can't have him. Even if the stars aligned and he decided he felt the same way, it would never work. There's too much history. Too much distrust.

I don't think I could ever look at him the way I did before he was arrested. Back then, he couldn't do any wrong. I think maybe that's why it was so hard for me to accept what he did. And again, it wasn't the drugs. Yes, I was hurt and shocked to find out he was caught dealing, especially given everything that happened with my mom, but it was that he involved Finn that hit me the hardest.

In that moment he had no regard for me or my future. A man that I would have literally died for, jeopardized everything I held dear so he could make a quick buck.

I know that's where all my anger stems from. That when it all boiled down, I simply did not matter enough. Even to this day the thought is debilitating.

Finn's right. I need to find a way to move past this. But not for Ryland. For myself. I have to find a way to let this go… To let *him* go. The way I should have done years ago.

Chapter 8

Ryland

"Fuck." I tear my hand out of the engine, seeing blood already running down my palm.

Not sure what I cut my finger on, I grab the roll of paper towels on the cart next to me and tear a couple off before wrapping them around the decent size cut that extends half the length of my index finger.

Today may have started out as a good day, but it quickly turned south. Starting when Ainsley showed up here with that Ken doll on her arm.

I've never seen her with a guy before. When I went away, she hadn't started dating yet. In fact, I don't ever remember her even expressing interest in anyone. At least not that she ever told me. But seeing her today with that guy, I don't know how to describe my feelings.

I'd like to say that it was just my protectiveness of her kicking in. That the only reason I wanted to smash that pretty boy's face in is because he's not good enough for Ainsley. And while that might be partially true, I know it's not the only reason I reacted the way I did.

I'd be lying if I said I hadn't looked at Ainsley when she was younger and thought about how pretty she was or how lucky the guy who ended up with her was going to be. But the thoughts were always in a brotherly way. Or so I thought.

But how I felt today? There was nothing brotherly about it. And the thought should bother me a hell of a lot fucking more than it does.

"Shit, dude. You okay?" Finn steps up next to me, his eyes swinging to the bloody paper towel wrapped around my finger.

"Yeah, just nicked it on something."

"Jim's got a first aid kit in the office. Go grab you a bandage." He nods his head in the direction of the back office.

"Yeah, I'll do that." I wait a beat before asking, "Did you see that guy Ains was with? He looked like a Ken doll."

"Right." Finn chuckles. "That's Matt. Not really sure what the deal is with them. Ainsley says their *just* friends. I'm not sure she would tell me if there was something else going on, though. She'd probably be afraid I'd scare him off."

"Would you?" I arch a brow at my best friend.

"Maybe." He shrugs. "I certainly didn't go easy on the last guy she brought around. Don't get me wrong, I want her to find someone. I want her to fall in love and be happy. But I don't want her to end up with some random dude that's not going to appreciate her, ya know? I want to make sure whoever she ends up with treats her like a fucking princess."

"Guys are assholes."

"That we are. I think about some of the shit you and I have pulled over the years. Fuck, if anyone treated Ainsley the way we've treated some of the females we've dated, I'd fucking lose it."

I don't vocalize it, but I feel the same way. Not that we were ever bad to any of them, per se. We just treated them more like objects than people. Fucked up, I know. But what do you really expect from two teenage guys who were raised to view women only one of two ways? Either they were family and you did everything to protect them. Or they were pussy and you fucked them.

I wish I could say we've grown out of that way of thinking, but truthfully, I don't know if we have. I haven't been out long enough to really know for myself, but I'm guessing Finn still operates by the same code. Or at least that's how it appeared at Moe's on Saturday night.

"Anyway, I don't want to think about that shit right now. I'm going to continue to believe that my baby sister will spend her entire life never having sex."

"Wishful thinking." I snort. "You can't possibly think she's still a virgin. She's twenty years old."

"Fuck, dude. Just stop." He shakes his head, his entire expression riddled in distaste. "So anyway, how's your first day going?" He jumps at the opportunity to change the subject.

"Pretty good. It's amazing to be working with my hands again."

While my stepdad may have been an abusive alcoholic, he knew his way around cars, and when he wasn't hitting me, he was teaching me how to work on them. I grew up with my hands covered in grease, and honestly, I loved it. So much so that shortly before I was locked up, I bought an old Chevelle that I was working on restoring.

Finn had it garaged for me after I got arrested but over time couldn't afford to keep paying the dude. I guess the garage owner ended up selling it to someone. It's not like Finn had any use for it, or anywhere to store it at his place. It didn't run so it wasn't really worth the trouble.

"Some of the guys are going next door to Ivy's for beers once we close. You interested?"

When I was in prison, beer was one of the things I missed the most. Not because I've ever been a heavy drinker – I haven't. I just really missed kicking back with the guys and throwing down a couple. It wasn't getting drunk that I missed but the act of holding a cold one in my hand while I laughed and fucked off with friends.

"Yeah, I could go for a beer," I agree, holding up my hand. "I'm gonna go see about getting something to put on this."

"Okay." Finn nods. "I've got one more service to do before I close down my station for the day. What about you?"

"I just have to finish this belt change and I think I'm good to go."

"Awesome. Meet me in the lobby when you're ready to head out."

"Will do." I wait until he's heading back to the other side of the garage before taking off toward the office.

"Fuck you, dude. It did not go down like that and you know it." Finn laughs, smacking the top of the bar table.

"Deny it all you want, but that's exactly how it happened. I think maybe you were too drunk to remember it clearly." I take a long pull of beer. "You were seriously sliding around like you had damn ice skates on your feet and were trying out for the fucking Olympic team. And you were getting into it, too." I snort out a laugh. "Doing this weird shit with your hands." I toss my arms up all dainty, giving my best impersonation of Finn from that night.

"Fuck, I wish I had witnessed this," Bill, one of the mechanics from the shop, chimes in. "Why didn't you record that shit? That would have been solid *gold* material."

"I wish I had thought to," I admit. "But what came next was even funnier." I give Finn a knowing look.

"Oh shit, what did he do?"

"It's what he *didn't* do that was so comical. Like how he didn't stay on his feet." I lean back in my chair, laughter causing my shoulders to shake. "In the middle of a spin, he completely lost it. Both of his feet came straight out from underneath him and his head smacked the road. If I hadn't been so worried that he'd just given himself a concussion, I probably would have been on the ground laughing at him. I can still remember the sound of his skull hitting the concrete. It wasn't until I knew he was okay that I really had a good laugh at his expense."

"And he's been laughing about it ever since," Finn grumbles next to me.

"I'm sorry, man. You thought you were a fucking ice skater." I laugh around the words.

"I was drunk."

"That's not an excuse for shit and you know it," Don interjects as he rejoins the table.

"Okay, well, how about this." Finn's sinister gaze slides to me. "I caught this guy playing dress up with my little sister." He hitches his thumb toward me. "And when I say dress up, I mean lipstick, eye shadow, the whole shebang. She even convinced him to prance around her room in a pair of our mom's old heels that she found in the attic."

"I never took you for a cross dresser." Don pokes fun at me.

"Shut up," I grumble. "She was eight. How was I supposed to tell her no?"

"Same way I always did. You just say no." Finn knocks his arm against mine. "This guy right here." He gestures toward me. "He'd throw down with the biggest and baddest of them all, but bring in Ainsley and he was like a squishy little puppet. She could get him to do anything."

"She was very persuasive," I argue, the thought of how much things have changed causing my chest to ache.

She could still probably get me to do anything, only now she doesn't want me to. She doesn't want anything from me. And I'm not ashamed to admit that it fucking hurts... A lot.

"I swear I've never seen a guy so wrapped around a girl's finger before," Finn continues.

"And man did she love him." I don't miss the way he says *did*. As in doesn't anymore. "Don't worry, man," he clasps me on the shoulder, "she'll come around," he reassures, clearly catching something in my expression.

"Yeah," I grunt, finishing off the remainder of my beer in one long pull.

"Well I know one thing for sure," Bill interjects. "That sister of yours sure is a knockout."

Both mine and Finn's eyes swing to Bill.

"Careful," I warn. "Pretty sure you're old enough to be her dad."

"That doesn't mean I can't appreciate a pretty girl when I see one." Bill holds his hands up. "I'm just saying."

"I'm with Bill," Jim, our boss, chimes in. "And I'm old enough to be her grandpa. So there." He chuckles.

"Not you, too," Finn grumbles.

"Sorry, Finn, but she really is a good-looking girl. Don't you think so, Ryland?"

Every set of eyes land on me and even though I think Ainsley is the most beautiful woman I've ever laid eyes on, it's not something I want to announce. Especially in front of Finn.

"She's pretty." I downplay my answer, nodding to the waitress when she points at my empty bottle.

"Not sure how she ended up with such an ugly brother though." Jim pokes Finn in the ribs.

"You guys keep talking about how pretty my sister is and I might need to find new friends to drink with," he warns, smiling as he lifts his beer bottle to his lips.

"If it makes you feel any better, I'm quite fond of Jim's daughter," Bill tacks on.

"You stay the hell away from Maureen." Jim wags a finger at him.

"Just keeping it real, Jimmy." He wiggles his eyebrows up and down.

Jim completely ignores him, his gaze honing in on me. "Speaking of pretty women, how's it been being out of prison?

"If I had to go five years without getting any, I think I'd screw anything with a pulse the first chance I got," Don interjects.

We all laugh in unison.

"It's been tough," I admit.

Fuck, it's been more than tough. Considering I didn't go more than a few weeks without it since I lost my virginity at fourteen, five years felt like a lifetime. And while I thought I'd go for the first woman available after I got out, that hasn't been the case.

I ignore why I think that is and turn my focus to the waitress as she sets a fresh beer down in front of me.

"Tough." Finn snorts. "You had two different women practically begging for it Saturday night and you ended up going home alone."

"I wasn't interested." I shrug, taking a drink of beer.

"What do you mean you weren't interested?" Bill leans forward, placing his elbows on the table. "Did she have a pulse?"

"Well, she was alive so I'm guessing so."

"Did she have a pussy?" Don joins the conversation.

"I mean, you can never be too sure these days, but yes, I believe so."

"Then what the fuck was the hold up?" Bill asks.

"Don't listen to these two," Jim intervenes, hitching his thumb in Don and Bill's direction. "They don't know what it's like to spend more than one night behind bars. There's an adjustment period. It takes a while to get your bearings and start to feel like yourself again."

"So then it's not just me?" I question.

"No." He shakes his head, threading his hands together in front of him. "I was so messed up after my stint in prison. It was nearly three months before I started to feel even a little bit like my old self."

I don't say it, but it feels good to hear. It's only been four days, and even though I feel like I should be ready to jump back into life, I don't. I'm out of prison and yet I feel like I'm still locked in the same tiny ass cell that I spent the last sixty-two months in.

"I told him it would take a while," Finn adds.

"I'll get there." I take another pull of beer. "For what it's worth, Jim, I really appreciate you giving me a shot. I don't think I actually said thank you; but thank you. I didn't expect to have a job so soon after getting out but it sure as shit made my probation officer happy."

"I know firsthand how hard it can be. I'm glad I could help out."

A brief silence passes between the five of us before Finn is climbing to his feet.

"Anyone up for a game of pool?" he asks, his gaze darting around the table.

"I'm game."

"Me, too." Bill adds.

"Oh hell, twist my arm," Jim grumbles, sliding out of his seat.

"You ladies have fun. I have to get home to the missus." Don finishes off his beer as he stands.

"Pussy whipped." Bill coughs.

"At least I have a pussy to whip me," Don fires back.

"Pretty sure he's got you there." Jim laughs.

After saying our goodbyes to Don, the rest of us spend the next hour shooting pool and bullshitting about nothing of any real importance. It feels good to be out, having drinks with the guys, but it does little to distract me from the nagging feeling that's been present in my stomach since earlier today when I watched Ainsley leave with that guy.

I know it shouldn't bother me. I know she's a grown woman and that she can take care of herself. But a part of me still feels responsible for her. And no matter how good of a guy he might be, I don't think anyone will be good enough for Ainsley. At least not in my eyes.

Finn drives us home shortly before ten. Knowing that he was driving, I allowed myself to drink a little bit more than I probably would have. I guess you could say I was attempting to drink my woes away. Not that it worked. I feel more conflicted now than when I sat down for that first beer.

Ainsley's car is in the driveway when we pull in which makes me feel mildly better. Of course I can't vocalize any of this to Finn because he'd probably think I'd lost my mind. Hell, maybe I have.

What else could explain my sudden obsession with his little sister? A girl I watched grow up. A girl I practically helped raise.

Some of the thoughts that have crossed my mind over the last couple of days, me from five years ago would beat my own ass right about now.

It's wrong on so many different levels and yet I can't help it. I can't help my attraction to her. I can't help the way my groin tightens every time she looks at me. And I sure as fuck can't help that she's the one thing that has plagued my dreams for the past three nights straight.

I've tried to reason with myself. Convince myself that I'm confusing my need to make things right with her as something more. But I know that's not it.

If I'm being completely honest with myself, and thanks to the eight beers I drank, I think I am. There's been something there with Ainsley since she was a teenager but because I knew I could never act on it, it kept me in check. It kept me in control.

But Ainsley isn't a child anymore. She's a woman. A fucking beautiful woman. And as such, my control is starting to slip. But I can't let it. Because no matter how strong the pull I feel toward her is, no matter how badly my body craves her, I know I could never be with her.

I've spent my whole life trying to protect her from the wrong kind of guy. It's a bitter pill to swallow when you realize that the wrong kind of guy is you.

Chapter 9

Ainsley

"Hey."

My eyes flutter open at the soft voice, landing on Finn who's hovering over the back of the couch looking down at me.

"Hey," I grumble out, my voice full of sleep. "I must have dozed off. What time is it?"

"Around ten. Why don't you go get in your bed?" He straightens his posture.

"Yeah, I think I will." I push back the throw blanket covering the lower half of my body before pushing myself up into a sitting position.

I rub my eyes with the backs of my hands, letting out a loud yawn.

I have no idea how long I've been asleep. I got home right after eight, and not having the energy to do any of the schoolwork I needed to, I plopped down on the couch, clicked on the television, and that's where I've been ever since.

It takes me a moment to find the strength to stand, but as soon as I do, my entire body protests the movement.

"Why were you out so late?" I ask, fumbling around the couch in my attempt to make it to the hallway.

I think maybe I'm still half asleep.

"We went out for drinks."

The comment has my eyes swinging back toward my brother, and only then do I realize that Ryland is standing next to him.

My heart instantly kicks up speed.

My body and head seem to be at odds where he's concerned and truthfully, the array of emotions is starting to become quite dizzying.

"Fun," I mutter, turning back toward the hallway.

"Well man, I think I'm gonna head that way as well," Ryland says behind me, a slight slur to his words. "I'm fucking beat."

"I'm gonna grab me a quick bite to eat and I won't be too far behind you," my brother responds as I reach the mouth of the hallway.

Knowing he isn't talking to me, I keep moving, reaching my bedroom door within seconds. Instead of pushing it open, I lay my forehead against the worn wood, pretty certain that I could fall asleep standing just like this. I'm that tired.

"What are you doing?" I hear Ryland approach, a hint of laughter to his words.

"I'm going to bed," I sleepily say.

"Pretty sure you have to open the door first." I feel him next to me, but I keep my head down and my eyes closed.

"I will… eventually." I let out another yawn.

"Here, let me help you." Before I have time to fully process what he's said, the door opens and I stumble forward. I no doubt would have landed flat on my face if not for the pair of arms that catch me around the waist just in the nick of time.

"Whoa." Ryland steadies me, pulling me upright.

"What the hell did you do that for?" I wiggle out of his grasp and turn on him, now wide awake.

"Sorry, I didn't think you'd just fall forward." He laughs.

"I was resting my eyes for a moment. I didn't realize you were going to open the door. I could have busted my head open." I flail my arms dramatically.

"And yet, you didn't," he points out.

"No thanks to you."

"No thanks to me? I'm the one that caught you."

"Yeah, after you opened the door which caused me to fall in the first place."

"Again, it's not like I knew you would fall."

"Ugh." The word gurgles in my throat. "Can you just go now so I can get in bed?"

"You sure you don't want me to tuck you in?" There's a boyish playfulness to his expression, and even though I'm mad, I smile.

"Are you drunk?" I place my hands on my hips and study him for a long moment.

"Maybe just a little." He holds his hand up and inches his thumb and index finger together until a bit of space separates them.

"Lord." I roll my eyes. "You realize it's Monday, right?"

"You realize I just got out of prison and I don't really care what day it is, right?" he fires back.

"Go to bed, Ryland." I point toward the hallway.

"You first." He grins and I'm not sure if I want to slap that grin off his face or take a picture of it so I can pull it out and look at it whenever I want.

"Out." I step toward him to push him out of my room, but when my hands connect with his solid chest, he doesn't budge. "Ryland, stop messing around. Get out." I try again, pushing into him with more weight. Still nothing.

"You're weaker than I remember," he tells me, pulling his bottom lip through his teeth in a way that makes my entire body take notice.

"And you're more infuriating than I remember."

"Well you're angrier than I remember." He grabs both of my wrists when I attempt to push him again. He lowers his face an inch from mine. "And so much more fucking beautiful," he whispers, our gazes locked.

My breathing accelerates as my heart begins to pound at rapid speed.

I open my mouth to say something, *anything*, but no words come out.

How can one sentence render me completely paralyzed? And yet, that's exactly what it's done.

It isn't until Finn's voice filters down the hall that my senses seem to return. I shake off Ryland's hold and take a full step back seconds before my brother appears behind Ryland in my doorway.

"What did you say?" I look around Ryland, trying to act as normal as possible.

"I asked what happened to all the cereal." His gaze darts from me to Ryland and then back to me.

"I got hungry earlier and finished what we had," I say, pulling the elastic band from my hair, the thick strands falling down my back as I turn toward my bed. "Now if you two don't mind, I have an early class tomorrow." I throw back my comforter and quickly climb underneath it.

"Goodnight," I say loudly when neither man has moved.

"Next time tell me when we're low on cereal." Finn spins around and Ryland quickly follows him into the hallway.

"Yeah, yeah," I call after him, laying back before pulling the blankets up to my chin.

When I glance back toward the door, Finn is gone but Ryland is still standing in the hallway.

"Will you flip the light off for me?" I ask, gesturing to the light switch next to the door.

He nods, leaning inside the doorframe to flip off the light. The room goes dark with the exception of the dim hall light that filters in behind Ryland.

He reaches for the doorknob and begins to pull it closed, stopping when there's only an inch to go. And that's when I hear his voice. It's so soft that for a moment I wonder if I'm hearing things.

"For what it's worth, Ains, I'm really sorry that I hurt you." With that, the door closes and I'm encased in darkness.

"Well. Well. Well. If it isn't Ainsley Kenter." Every hair on the back of my neck stands at the sound of the man's voice behind me. It's a voice I would recognize anywhere.

I whip around in the middle of the sidewalk outside of Milo's where I've just finished my evening shift.

"Oscar?" I stutter, my stomach twisting as I take in his appearance. He's just as good-looking as I remember. Dark hair, rugged features, amazing body, but unfortunately that's where his pleasantries end.

He's wearing his customary athletic apparel that he always used to wear. Loose fitting gym shorts, a black OSU t-shirt, and a backward baseball cap.

"What...what are you doing here?" I try to pretend not to be completely thrown by seeing him here. It's been over two years since he left for college to play baseball and I haven't spoken a word to him since.

"We have a tournament against WSU that starts tomorrow. I was planning on coming by to see you but it looks like you saved me the trip." He smiles which causes the sick feeling in my stomach to multiply.

To most, I'm sure Oscar seems like the average all-American college student. But to those of us who know him well, we see beyond the façade he works very hard to keep in place.

Unfortunately, this wasn't always the case for me. I was one of the blind ones. One of the people that fell for his lies and easy smile. It wasn't until it was already too late that I finally saw his true colors. And what I saw terrified me to my core.

Oscar was my first real boyfriend. We dated for a few months our senior year of high school. And while Finn didn't really care for him, I had been blinded by his good looks and popularity.

Things were amazing those first couple of months, but after we slept together for the first time, something in him shifted. He became extremely possessive and controlling. I couldn't talk to another guy without him going into a rage and accusing me of cheating.

Eventually, it got so bad that I ended things between us. Although, that did little to deter him. He'd show up at my house, at work, when I was out to dinner with friends. It was like everywhere I turned, there he was.

The more I pushed him away, the more he pushed back. It's like he couldn't accept that I didn't want to be with him. After a while things started to get physical. He didn't hit me or anything. He knew better than to leave a mark. But that doesn't mean he didn't shove me around, restrain me, or even go as far as to pin me against a wall with his hand wrapped tightly around my throat once.

It wasn't until I threatened to go to the police that he backed off. Even still, he never completely went away. That is until he landed himself a baseball scholarship at Ohio State University.

It's been two years since he left, and the day he got into his car and drove away was probably one of the best days of my life. It felt like a thousand-pound weight had been lifted off my shoulders.

"Oh, well I probably wouldn't have been home anyway. I'm not there very often. You know, work and school and all," I reply after a long moment passes.

"You always were the overachiever." He rocks back on his heels. "But you're free now, right?"

"Huh?"

"You're free now, right? We should catch up. You want to go grab a hot chocolate from Anne's like we used to?"

"It's a little warm out for hot chocolate." I push out a breath, swallowing past the hard lump in my throat. "Besides, I can't tonight. I have plans."

"Plans? With who?" His gaze darkens.

"With Finn." I force an easy smile. "I've been so busy recently that we've started setting aside certain evenings to have dinner together."

"Oh, I see." His features instantly relax. "What about tomorrow?"

"I'm actually pretty full all week. I've got finals coming up next week and I have a lot of studying to get done." I shrug, trying to seem a little disappointed in hopes of appeasing him.

"Seriously, Ainsley." His forehead creases. "You can't give me an hour?"

"I wish I could. I really do." I start to back away. "Maybe next time, yeah?"

"Next time?"

"It was really great seeing you," I lie, throwing up a half wave before quickly spinning around.

I make a beeline for my car parked across the street, glancing over my shoulder a couple times to make sure he doesn't follow me. Surprisingly he doesn't.

When I pull out onto the street less than a minute after reaching my car, Oscar is still standing on the sidewalk, his eyes on me as I drive away.

I call Lily on the way home and am still sitting in my driveway venting to her fifteen minutes after I've arrived. She doesn't know Oscar personally, but our friendship began shortly before he left town so she knows *about* him. In fact, she's the only person that really knows anything about what went on between the two of us. I kept most things to myself as it was happening. I don't know why. I guess I was ashamed, though I now know I had absolutely nothing to be ashamed of. Well, other than the fact that I let him fool me into believing he was someone he wasn't and in turn, I ended up losing my virginity to him. Which is something I regret to this day.

Seeing Oscar really threw me today, and even though Lily manages to calm me down a bit, my stomach is still one big knot as I hang up the phone and head inside.

Finn and Ryland are lounging on the couch as I enter. My knee jerk reaction is to slide in between them, a place where I've always felt safe, and tell them everything. If anyone can make Oscar leave me alone for good, it's these two. Or at least, it used to be these *two*. I guess Ryland isn't really part of that equation anymore.

I immediately push the thought away. Just because Oscar is in town doesn't mean he's going to start in with his old antics. It's been two years, for goodness' sake. Certainly he's moved on by now. And again, he's only here for a tournament, I remind myself.

"Hey." Finn barely looks up from the television as I enter.

"Hey."

"How was work?"

"It was work." I shrug, keeping my back to both men as I kick my shoes off next to the door.

"I ran to the store earlier so there's some lunchmeat in the fridge if you're hungry. I also bought some of those rice cups you like so much."

"I ate at the restaurant but thank you." I turn, keeping my eyes forward as I make my way across the living room. "I've got a lot of schoolwork to catch up on so if you need me I'll be in my room," I say, not waiting for a response as I duck down the hallway toward my bedroom.

For a solid two hours I try and fail to get any work done. I keep re-reading the same paragraph over and over again without retaining a single piece of information. By ten o'clock I completely give up, resigning to the fact that I'm not going to get any studying in tonight.

Despite my lack of appetite, I decide I should probably try to eat a little something before I go to bed. I'd lied to Finn earlier. I didn't eat at work. I just needed a quick escape because one look at me and he would have known something was up.

The rest of the house is quiet as I enter the living room. The television is off and it would appear that everyone has turned in for the night. Relieved, I head toward the kitchen.

While the main light is off, I see a soft light filtering in through the back door. Figuring someone must have left the porch light on, I cross the room, preparing to shut it off. But just as I reach the switch, something outside catches my eye.

Ryland…

He's sitting on the back step, his knees pulled to his chest, his face turned up toward the sky. I take a moment to look at him while no one is around. The broadness of his shoulders, the profile of his handsome face, the messy layers of hair that fall in every direction on his head. Despite everything, the sight of him momentarily steals my breath.

Before I realize what I'm doing, my hand is on the doorknob and seconds later I'm pulling it open. Ryland's head swings in my direction as I step outside, his expression a mixture of surprise and concern.

"What are you doing sitting out here by yourself?" I ask, pulling the door closed behind me.

Ryland's eyes follow me as I sit down next to him.

"Just thinking." He sighs.

"Thinking about what?" I ask, looking up at the starless sky. The cloud coverage is too thick for a single one to shine through.

"Nothing. Everything." He shrugs. "What about you? I thought you were studying."

"I tried. I failed." I blow out a puff of air, wrapping my arms around myself.

While it's warm through the day, the nights are still quite chilly. It doesn't help that I'm only wearing a thin pair of pajama bottoms and a tank top.

"Here." Ryland shifts next to me. I look over to see him tug his hoodie over his head. "Put this on." He shoves it at me.

"That's okay."

"Ainsley." He gives me a look, one that I've seen countless times over the course of my life.

"Fine." I huff, knowing he won't take no for an answer.

Taking the sweatshirt, I quickly slide it on, Ryland's scent overwhelming me the instant I do. I have to resist the urge to snuggle my face down into the fabric and breathe him in as deeply as I can.

Old habits die hard.

"Having trouble concentrating?" he asks once I'm warmly nestled in his hoodie.

"Huh?"

"You said you tried to study and you failed. Something on your mind?"

"You could say that." I have to stop myself from elaborating.

"Anything you want to talk about?"

"Not really," I admit, my gaze going back up to the night sky. "I'd just like to sit here for a minute if that's okay with you."

"Of course." I see his head nod in my peripheral vision but I keep my attention focused upward.

We sit in silence for several minutes. Neither of us talking, both of us lost to our own thoughts. It's something I've done with Ryland a thousand times before. Even when I was young. If I was ever feeling anxious or worried about something, just existing in the same space with him would make me feel better. I guess it's kind of reassuring to know he still has that effect on me.

As my mind wanders, I wonder why I'm still so angry at him. Why I'm holding onto something he did so many years ago. It's his life and he made his own choices. Is that really a reason for me to shut him out of my life forever?

I can see he's trying. And I know this is hard for him. He doesn't have to tell me; I can read him that well. Knowing that after five years apart I still feel like I know him that well is a little surprising yet comforting at the same time.

Then again, after everything that happened, I found myself questioning if I knew him at all.

But this… this connection. This unspoken moment passing between us makes me question myself for ever thinking such things.

Ryland may have made a very questionable choice – one that not only affected his life, but mine and Finn's as well – but he's still Ryland. The same guy who held me for hours the night my father died. The same guy who used to take me to the park in the dead of winter when Finn refused to. The one who would turn our entire living room into one gigantic fort because I wanted to camp out in the backyard but my dad wouldn't let me.

He's been here through everything. Every up and down. Every high and low. He was my rock. Until he left me…

But he's here now. He's here and he's trying, isn't he? I think about the whispered apology he offered me as he closed my bedroom door the other night. Even slurred from his inebriation there was still so much honesty in those words.

Maybe I'm fooling myself. Maybe Oscar showing up today has got my head all out of whack. But I can't help but believe him.

I believe that he's sorry and I have no doubt that he'd walk through fire to prove it to me.

You can't fake the kind of relationship Ryland and I had. You can't fake the time we spent together or the fact that he's been a part of my family for my entire life. Even though I never told him how I truly felt about him, our relationship was always the most honest one I ever had.

I may have withheld certain information, but I never lied to him. I never tried to hide who I was. And he accepted me in a way no one ever had before or has since.

If I'm being honest with myself, there's been a huge hole in my life since he left and I've been trying so hard to fill it that I didn't realize until this very moment that there was never any way of filling it. There's no one that could ever take his place.

"Can I ask you something?" I finally break the silence after what feels like hours.

"Anything."

Our eyes meet and a bolt of electricity shoots through me.

"What's your biggest regret?"

I watch his expression soften as he stares back at me.

"Truthfully?"

I nod, waiting for him to continue.

"I have a lot of them. I regret what happened the day I got arrested and I've regretted most of the decisions I've made since, but I think my biggest regret, and one that I'll never be able to fully apologize for, is leaving you."

My breath catches in my throat.

"I spent years promising you that I'd always be here for you. And then I turned around and did something that took me away from you for far too long. I'll never forgive myself for lying to you, even though that was never my intention."

"I was mad," I admit. "I was mad at what you did. Knowing how my mom suffered with addiction. For you to turn around and deal drugs, was like a slap in the face. But then to involve Finn."

"You know I would never have intentionally put Finn in harm's way," he interjects.

"I can see that now, yes. But at the time it didn't feel that way."

"I get that." He blows out a hard breath.

"But I think the thing that hurt the most was that you left."

"You know I would have stayed if I could have."

"I know." I hold his gaze, even though doing so feels almost impossible. "I'm sorry I never came to see you. I was so angry for so long…"

"Please, Ains. Do not apologize to me for anything. You did nothing wrong."

"Even still, I let my anger lead the charge. It was easier that way. It was easier to be angry than admit to myself how devastated I was that you were gone."

"Ainsley." He reaches for my hand, pulling it into his lap before wrapping his fingers around it. My skin warms from his touch.

"I'm not saying that all is forgiven. I'm not promising that things will magically be okay with us again. But I want to try to move on. Carrying around this anger isn't helping either of us. I just want things to go back to the way they used to be," I admit in a moment of weakness. "Or at least as normal as they can be."

"So do I." He smiles at me, and for the first time since he's been home, the action lights up his entire face.

Knowing I had something to do with that leaves me feeling a way I'm fairly certain I haven't felt since before he left.

"Well." I pull my hand away, feeling like I need to break up the moment before it becomes too heavy and I end up professing my lifelong love to him. "I should probably head back inside. I have an early class in the morning."

"Yeah, of course." He clears his throat, standing at the same time I do.

"I'll see you tomorrow?" I ask.

"Tomorrow." He nods.

"Goodnight, Ryland." I turn, pulling open the backdoor.

"Goodnight, Ainsley," I hear him say moments before I step inside the warm kitchen.

I abandon my need for food as I quickly head toward my bedroom, my heart beating so fast and hard I feel out of breath by the time I reach it.

Once in my room, I realize I'm still wearing Ryland's sweatshirt, and while I know I should take it back out to him, I can't bring myself to part with it just yet.

Climbing into bed, I pull the blanket up around me as I nuzzle into Ryland's hoodie, letting myself get lost in his scent.

An hour ago I felt nervous and anxious over everything. Ryland. Oscar. School. All of it. But as I close my eyes and drift off to sleep, I feel more at peace than I have in a very long time.

I guess that should be my first indicator that making amends with Ryland was the right thing to do. My life hasn't felt the same since he left and I don't think anything will feel okay again until we're okay. So, despite everything that's happened, I need to find a way to make us right again.

I owe it to the little girl who worshipped him and to the woman who still loves him, in spite of everything he's done.

Chapter 10

Ainsley

Five years ago...

I pace back and forth across the front lawn of my school. Ryland was supposed to be here to pick me up over an hour ago and still hasn't shown. I waited inside for a while, but eventually was forced outside when Ms. Ilg needed to lock up the school and head home.

She offered to give me a ride, but I reassured her that my ride would be here any minute. That was a half an hour ago.

I stay late nearly every Thursday to utilize the school's extensive library. It's one of the nicest features of our school. And every Thursday at five o'clock, Ryland is here to pick me up. Which is why I'm starting to panic. He's so late and neither he nor Finn are picking up their cell phones.

When I see a dark truck pull into the lot, a wave of relief runs through me.

Finally.

Only when the passenger window rolls down I see that it's not Ryland in the driver's seat.

"Charlotte?" I question, confused as to why Ryland's cousin has his truck and why she's here and not him.

"Get in." She jerks her chin.

I hesitate for a brief moment before doing as she says, quickly climbing into Ryland's truck.

"What are you doing here? Where's Ryland?" I ask, concern evident in my voice as I drop my book bag on the floorboard and quickly snap my seatbelt into place.

"He and Finn are at the police station," she says, quickly pulling out of the parking lot.

"What do you mean they're at the police station?" I gape in her direction.

"Exactly what I said. They're at the police station. They've been arrested."

Charlotte is a little rough around the edges. The kind of girl that dresses in all black, has tattoos and piercings galore, and doesn't have a bullshit bone in her body. She's straight and to the point, no matter what's going on. Which sometimes isn't always a good thing, and partly why Ryland has very little to do with her. She's someone you can only take in small doses. But right now, her unapologetic honesty is exactly what I need.

"Arrested?" I choke out, still not sure I heard her right. *"Why would they be arrested?"*

"I don't know all the details. Something about a drug deal and an undercover cop. He didn't have much time to explain. He only got one short phone call and he opted to call me after Finn couldn't reach you. He asked me to pick you up and take you home. He said he'd call later with more information."

My mind drifts back to the unknown call I received shortly after I arrived in the library. I ignored it, as I usually do. Ninety-nine percent of the time it's either spam or a wrong number. And since he didn't leave a message…

"Wait. Did you say drug deal?*" My mind swirls back through what all she just told me.*

I feel like I'm moving at a snail's pace. Like everything is coming at me in rapid fire but my brain isn't able to process it at the same speed.

"I'm not sure what happened. I told you pretty much everything I know."

"And Finn. He's there, too." I need to confirm, because this isn't possible.

"That's what Ryland said. I was given specific instructions to drive you home and to stay with you until Finn arrived."

"Stay with me. Why would you need to stay with me?"

"Look, kid, I don't know. All I know is that Ryland was pretty riled up and was adamant that you are not to be left alone."

Despite everything she's telling me, and that being alone is probably the last thing I need to be, I think I'd prefer it over being forced to stay with a woman who clearly doesn't possess an ounce of compassion.

I'm on the verge of a panic attack and she has the nerve to be aggravated at me for asking questions. I never questioned the reason why I didn't like her, but the feeling has grown substantially over the last two minutes.

Afraid to ask anything more, I sit in twisted silence for the remainder of the fifteen-minute drive home. When we pull into my driveway, I can't get out of the truck fast enough.

Unfortunately, once inside, things don't get any better. I pace the living room, checking my phone every two minutes, while Charlotte lounges on the couch flipping through a magazine like she doesn't have a care in the world.

I'm so infuriated with her behavior and lack of knowledge or care about what's going on that I have to stop myself from laying into her several times over the course of the evening.

I've worried myself so sick that I've become physically ill twice, my stomach so out of sorts that I'm not able to hold anything down. Something that's only made a hell of a lot worse by my present company.

When the front door opens right after nine, I nearly jump out of my skin. I take off toward the front of the house, practically plowing into Finn as he enters the living room.

"Where the hell have you been?" I wrap my arms around his torso, squeezing him with every ounce of power I have in me. "Charlotte said you were arrested." I pull back, ready to demand answers.

"Charlotte should learn to keep her mouth shut and follow instructions." Finn throws an angry glare her way.

"Hey, he said to pick her up and stay with her." She pushes to a stand. "I'm here, aren't I?"

"And clearly only making things worse. You can go now." Finn's tone holds an unbelievable amount of annoyance and anger.

"Tell Ryland the next time he needs help to call someone else." She snags her jacket off the back of the couch and stalks toward the door.

"Don't worry. I will," Finn snarls, his gaze locked on her as she exits the house without another word.

He waits a few long seconds before turning back to me, by which time I feel even more confused about what the hell is going on.

"Have you eaten? Are you hungry?" He looks me over with concern.

"I'm more concerned with where you've been."

"Come on." He hooks an arm over my shoulder and guides me into the kitchen. "I'll make you something to eat."

"Finn, I'm fifteen. If I was hungry, I could have made something for myself. Now stop stalling and tell me what the hell is going on. Why were you in jail and where is Ryland?" I demand, pushing his arm off of my shoulder as I turn to face him.

Finn runs a hand through his hair, blowing out a heavy breath as he tries to find the right words.

"Ryland and I had some errands to run. He told me he had a package to drop off on the way. I thought nothing of it. Turns out the package was a large duffle bag full of prescription drugs."

"That can't be right. Ryland would never sell drugs," I interject, finding this information so preposterous I can't even begin to entertain that it might be true.

"The guy he was selling to turned out to be an undercover cop. He arrested Ryland on the spot and me right along with him."

"Wait." I stop him, not able to ignore the feeling in my gut that he's not giving me the full truth. "He arrested you both?"

"Because I was with Ryland, he assumed I knew what was in the bag. But I didn't. Until they could investigate further, they took us both to the station. It wasn't until Ryland insisted I had no knowledge of it that they finally decided to let me go."

"And Ryland?"

"No idea." He shakes his head, his expression more conflicted than I think I've ever seen it. "The officer who released me said they'll set a court appearance sometime in the next day or two, and that official charges will be filed at that time."

"So he's stuck in there?" My instinct is to go to him. To find a way to help him. I haven't even stopped for one second to consider what he's done. Only that he's not here and I need him with me. "For how long? How long will he be there, Finn?"

"He's looking at some pretty serious charges, Ains." He reaches around and squeezes the back of his neck.

"What kind of charges? How long is he going to be in there?" I fire off questions without waiting for a response.

"I don't know."

"How long, Finn?" I stomp my foot, my temper flaring.

"From what the officer told me, he could be facing somewhere around ten years."

"Ten years?" I stumble backward, my head spinning.

"He may not get that. We will just have to see what the official charges are. Ryland's never been in any real trouble before. Maybe the judge will go easy on him."

"Ten years," I repeat, unable to process anything else.

"It's possible." Finn's shoulders sag forward as he slides down into one of the old, wooden kitchen chairs.

I numbly take the seat across from him, knowing deep in my gut that I won't be seeing Ryland again for a very, very long time. And the thought is downright paralyzing.

Chapter 11

Ainsley

"So that's it? You two are friends again?" Lily asks, following me to the drink station behind the bar.

"I wouldn't say we're friends," I correct her. "But I am trying to let go of the past."

"Well, for what it's worth, I think you're doing the right thing. Carrying around grudges only weighs you down. And you, my dear, carry enough weight as it is."

"Is that your way of calling me fat?" I laugh, filling two glasses with ice before setting them on the counter. Reaching for the handheld soda dispenser, I fill one cup with Sprite and the other with Coke.

"Oh shut up. You know that's not what I meant." She playfully smacks my arm, causing liquid to spill over the side of one of the glasses I've picked up. "I'm just saying, you are the most stressed out twenty-year-old I've ever met. Anything you can do to lessen the load is for the better."

"The most stressed out?" I quirk a brow at her.

"Don't look at me like it's not true. You know it is." Lily's eyebrow raises.

"Well if you'll excuse me, this stress ball needs to get these drinks to her table." I slide past her and around the counter, heading back into the dining room.

Lily and I have been discussing my conversation with Ryland in short intervals over the course of our five-hour shift. Because we haven't had any real time to sit down and talk, I've filled her in with bits and pieces as the evening has progressed. She seems to be happy with my decision to forgive Ryland, and honestly so am I.

I feel lighter today than I have in a very long time. And I think it's because I've finally admitted to myself that it wasn't just Ryland that screwed up all those years ago. It was me, too. Because while he may have made a very questionable choice that landed him in a world of trouble, I was the one that turned my back on him when he needed me the most.

"So, does this mean I can come over and check out *your* hottie more often now that you two have kissed and made up?" Lily asks after I've returned from my table and am busy entering their order into the computer system.

"One, we did not *kiss* and make up," I say, no matter how much I can't deny that I wish we had. I shake off the thought. "And two, no, you cannot come over to ogle him. So, unless you're offering your services in the way of finals studying, you are not allowed to come over until my exams are out of the way next week," I tell her, laughing when she pulls in a dramatic breath and steps back like I've truly offended her.

"And here I thought we were best friends."

"We are." I chuckle. "And as such, it is your job to help me stay on task, not distract me with your shenanigans."

"Shenanigans." She scoffs.

"Are you denying that you're the queen of distractions?" I gesture to the computer, trying to make my point.

"Ugh." She groans. "You are no fun."

"If I wasn't so concerned with everything else I have going on, I might be offended by that statement. But right now, I can't argue it. The time for fun will be at the end of finals."

"At which time, I'm coming over with a bottle of tequila and we are going to celebrate."

"Oh no you don't." I send my order through and turn toward her. "The last time we celebrated with tequila, I spent two days nursing the world's worst hangover."

I have been drunk a total of two times in my life. Both times were at the hands of Lily, and both times left me hugging the toilet at the end of the night. I blame her love of hard liquor. Maybe I need to find a new drinking buddy.

"And?" She crosses her arms in front of herself.

"And, I have no desire to repeat it."

"Well, unfortunately for you, I'm a horrible listener." She smiles so wide it nearly splits her face apart.

"Ainsley, Lily, get back to work." We both turn in unison to see the shift manager Kevin watching us from the window of the kitchen.

"Yes, boss." Lily rocks up onto her tiptoes before turning, throwing me a playful wink, and sauntering off toward the dining room.

I roll my eyes and shake my head, stuffing my order tablet back into the front pocket of my apron before following after her to check on my tables while I wait for my last two orders to come up.

"Longest shift ever," Lily groans as we exit the restaurant right after nine. "Seriously. Is it just me or does it feel like these shifts keep getting slower?"

"It probably doesn't help that you insist on looking at the clock every five minutes. Haven't you ever heard the saying about boiling water?"

"No? What saying?" she asks, following me across the street where both of our cars are parked.

"The one where…" My words die in my throat when I turn and see Oscar jogging across the street after us.

"The one where…" Lily prompts me to continue before registering the look on my face. She turns to see what I'm looking at right as Oscar reaches us.

"Hey, Ainsley. I was just having dinner with some friends and I saw you come out. Thought I'd come say hi." He gives me almost the exact same excuse he did yesterday when we ran into each other at the end of my shift.

"Oh, that's nice." I have to fight to roll my eyes. "Where were you guys eating?"

"Just over there." He points in the direction of the café but doesn't name a specific place. My bullshit meter starts pinging like crazy.

"Lily, this is Oscar," I say in a way I know she'll understand but he likely won't pick up on.

Her eyes widen slightly but then an easy smile slides across her face.

"Hi, Oscar." She turns, offering him her hand. "I'm Lily."

"It's a pleasure, Lily." He turns on the same charm that once had me eating out of the palm of his hand, but now sours my stomach. He shakes her hand and then releases it, his gaze swinging back to me. "What are you up to tonight? Got time to hang out for a little while."

"Actually, Lily and I were getting ready to head back to my place to study," I lie, knowing Lily will cover for me.

"Oh cool. You need any extra help?" he offers, which I suspected he would.

"No, we've got it. You should get back to your friends." I try to keep my responses light and carefree, even though on the inside I feel the lines tightening.

"Yeah." His expression falls. "Okay, then." He takes a step back. "Tomorrow maybe?"

"I wish I could, but I have class tomorrow." It's the truth, but even if I was free there's no way I would agree to hang out with him

"Well, if you change your mind I'd love to see you." He lets me off easy because Lily is here. Otherwise he probably wouldn't be so understanding.

"Okay. I'll keep that in mind." I throw up an awkward wave as he turns and jogs back across the street. I try to watch where he goes but I lose sight of him after he passes Milo's.

"What are the odds that he just happens to be coming out of a restaurant with his parents one night and his friends the next night, both times as your shift is ending?" Lily pulls my attention back to her, her mind clearly going in the exact same direction as mine.

"My thoughts exactly."

"You need to be careful while he's in town. He may not be a threat to you a state away, but he's clearly still holding onto some kind of hope where you're concerned. Best not to ruffle his feathers too much while he's here."

"I'm trying not to." I blow out a puff of air.

"Well, until he's gone I don't think you should be going anywhere alone. Even if it's just me tagging along with you."

"Agreed." I nod, unlocking my car door before pulling it open. It squeals per usual.

"Call me when you're home and don't stop anywhere," she tells me, unlocking her own car door.

"Yes, ma'am." I give her a smile and a wave before sliding into the driver's seat.

"Knock, knock." I rap lightly against Ryland's bedroom door. Because it's not latched, the door swings open and I'm offered the full view of Ryland, stretched out in his bed, his back propped against the headboard, reading a book of all things.

"Hey." He looks up from the paperback in his hands.

"Hey." I smile, gesturing to his book. "Am I seeing things or is Ryland Thorpe reading a book right now?" I chuckle, taking a few steps into the room.

"Busted." He laughs, sitting up further before dropping the book face down on top of the bed.

"I'm sorry to interrupt, I just wanted to return this." I hold up my arm which has Ryland's hoodie draped over it.

"Oh, okay. Thank you. You can just toss it there." He gestures to the end of the bed.

I take a few more steps into the room, stopping to deposit the sweatshirt where he indicated.

"What are you reading?" I point toward the book, not able to make out the title given how worn the cover is.

"It's called *438 Days*." He glances down at the book. "It's about a man who survived alone at sea for four hundred and thirty-eight days. It's really quite interesting."

"It sounds like it." I nod. "I didn't realize you liked to read."

"I don't, or well, I didn't. But when you're stuck in a tiny cell for hours a day there's only so much you can do to pass the time. I found that I actually really like to read. It offers an escape of sorts. I guess that's why I used to catch you with your nose in a book." He grins and I swear my heart physically skips a beat.

"Yeah." I shuffle my feet. "I haven't read for pleasure in a very long time. I've found that having to read over notes and countless textbooks has stolen my desire to pick up a book these days."

"Maybe you should force yourself. You never know, you may find it's exactly what you need."

"Maybe." I hesitate, my eyes scanning my father's old bedroom. It's almost exactly as it was when my dad was alive, other than some new bedding and the boxes piled in the corner that Ryland must have pulled from storage.

When Ryland was arrested he was still living with his mom and stepdad. They pretty much told him that if someone didn't come get his stuff from their house they were going to set it out on the curb. Finn went over the next day and collected the important stuff and stored it in our attic.

I'm honestly surprised he even went to his parents' house when he was released. His mom was always a selfish beast and his stepdad was even worse. I can't imagine either have changed that much in the last five years. And given that he showed up on our front porch shortly after he went there, I'm guessing I'm right in that assumption.

When he was a teenager, I remember him staying here for weeks on end after he and his stepfather would get into it. I can't count how many times Ryland had a black eye or busted lip growing up. Probably more times than I even know.

"Feels weird, doesn't it?" he asks, pulling my gaze back to him. "Me being in here. Still feels like Brian's room, doesn't it?" He seems to know exactly what I'm thinking at this exact moment.

"A little," I admit. "I haven't spent much time in here since he died."

"Yeah, I can understand. I don't know." He shrugs, looking around the room. "Makes me feel kind of close to him. You know how much I cared for your dad." When his gaze comes back to me there's sadness behind his eyes.

"I know." I knot my hands in front of myself. "Well, I guess I'll let you get back to your book."

"You could stay." Ryland stops me before I've managed to move a single inch. "You used to read to me all the time, even the most farfetched bunch of BS ever. It might be nice to have me read to you for a change."

"I shouldn't. I have a lot of stuff to do."

"Oh come on." He scoots over, patting the bed next to him. "Who knows, you might actually like it."

I look at him for a long moment, battling between what I want to do and what I know I should do – neither of which are lining up with the other.

"Fine," I grumble after a long moment. Crossing around the bed, I climb in next to Ryland, mirroring his position as I rest my back against the headboard. "But if it's awful I'm leaving."

"Deal." He smiles, picking the book back up. His eyes scan the page, finding where he was before he begins to read aloud.

"Ains." His voice is like a dream. A dream I never want to wake up from. "Ainsley." I feel his hand on my shoulder, followed by a light shake. "Hey." Ryland smiles the instant my eyes flutter open. "You fell asleep." He chuckles. "Guess my book wasn't that good after all."

"No, it was." I push up on my elbow, realizing that I must have moved in my sleep, considering I'm curled on my side rather than propped up against the headboard. "I guess I was just really tired." I shift, pushing myself the rest of the way up. "What time is it?"

"Almost one."

"In the morning?" I glance at the clock on the bedside table to confirm. "How long was I asleep?"

"About three hours. You seemed so peaceful I couldn't bear to wake you right away, so I let you sleep while I finished my book."

"How was it?" I ask, throwing my legs over the side of the bed as I stretch out. "The book, I mean?"

"It was really good, actually. You fell asleep right as it was getting to the good part."

"Yep. That sounds like me." I yawn, pushing to my feet.

"I would have let you sleep here all night but I thought it might freak you out to wake up in here in the morning. And truth be told, I selfishly didn't want to sleep on the couch."

"No, I'm glad you woke me," I lie, knowing I would take sleeping next to Ryland over sleeping alone in my own room any day of the week. Then again, if he's on the couch it kind of negates the point.

"I thought about carrying you to your room but then I thought I probably shouldn't."

"It's not like you haven't done it hundreds of times before."

"Yeah, but that was different. You're not a little girl anymore. And to be frank, I worried it might be overstepping. You only just started talking to me again. I'd hate to fuck that up by pushing too hard too fast."

"Well, I appreciate you being so considerate." I turn toward the door. "And thank you for tonight." I take in his rumpled hair and wrinkled shirt and all I want to do is climb right back in that bed with him. "It was nice to shut my brain off for a while."

"Literally." He chuckles, reminding me of the fact that I fell asleep.

"Yes, but while I was awake also. Maybe next time you can read me something a little more action packed." I smile.

"I'd love that."

"Well, goodnight." I head toward the door, knowing if I don't force myself to leave now I may not leave at all.

"Goodnight, Ainsley," he says moments before the door snaps closed.

I turn to head to my room, but my entire body freezes when Finn exits the bathroom at the exact same moment and catches me coming out of Ryland's room. His eyes dart to the door behind me and then back to my face.

"Ryland was reading me a book," I say, realizing how silly my explanation sounds.

Ryland Thorpe, badass of all badasses, reading me a bedtime story. I nearly laugh at the thought.

"He was reading you a book," Finn repeats each word slowly.

"Some book about a guy who was adrift for like four hundred days or something on the ocean. I wish I could tell you more but I fell asleep." I try to act like it's no big deal, as my feet finally remember how to work and I take the few short steps to my bedroom door.

"Gotcha." A slow smile turns up Finn's lips.

"What?" I arch a brow at him. "Why are you looking at me like that?"

"Nothing." He immediately wipes the smile from his face. "It's just good to see you two finding some semblance of normal again," he admits. "Though if I remember right, usually you're the one reading."

"Apparently Ryland is a reader now. Who knew?" I shrug my shoulders. "Well, goodnight." I shove my door open and quickly step inside.

"Goodnight." Finn chuckles, the floor creaking under his feet as he heads back down the hallway.

Chapter 12

Ryland

"So I was thinking, maybe we should plan a little celebratory dinner for Ainsley tonight." Finn appears next to the car I'm working on. "Today is her last exam and I know how stressed she's been. Plus, she's officially a senior now. That's something to celebrate, right? My sister, a soon to be college graduate. Who would have thought?"

"Pretty sure we all knew it was coming," I point out, grabbing a wrench from my work cart.

"I know. I'm just saying, she's the first Kenter to go to college…maybe ever. And now here she is, about to start her final year."

"You look like a proud papa bear."

"I am proud. Hell, I'm more than proud. She may have been a pain in the ass for most of my life, but she's *my* pain in the ass. To see her succeed after everything means a lot, man."

"I know. I'm pretty proud of her myself."

"You two seem to have been getting along pretty nicely this past week. Am I to assume that things are good on that front?"

"We're getting there. I think she's still hesitant but every day that passes I feel like we get a little closer to breaking down those walls."

"See, I told you." He clasps my shoulder. "I knew she'd come around eventually."

I nod.

Finn may have been confident, but I certainly was not. I know the issues Ainsley has with abandonment. And at the end of the day, despite everything else, I think she's made it pretty clear that that's where her anger stemmed from. She felt abandoned by someone she thought she could count on.

I hurt her. Even though that's the last thing I wanted to do. Hell, that's why I did what I did. I knew there would be blow back, but I was willing to take it if it meant that she was safe and with her brother.

I wanted to be able to salvage what little childhood she had left and I like to think in some ways, that's exactly what I did.

But the Ainsley I left is not the Ainsley I came home to. That was apparent the moment I walked in the door the day I was released. And the more time I spend with her, the more I realize just how much she's changed.

Sure, she's still Ainsley at her core. The same girl I've known and loved since before she could talk. But there are new parts to her, too.

Parts of her that I'm still getting to know. Parts that I'm finding draw me to her even more than I already am. And with that I find my attraction for her grows as well.

I know how fucked up it is to pine after your best friend's little sister, trust me, I do. It's even more fucked up that she's always been like *my* little sister. But when I look at her, I don't see the same sweet and innocent little girl I used to. In her place is an irresistible young woman who has consumed my thoughts for days on end.

When she's near, it takes everything in me not to touch her. When she's away, it's impossible not to be thinking of her. And while I know nothing could ever happen between us, it certainly hasn't stopped me from wishing it could.

"So what do you say?" Finn interrupts my thoughts, pulling me back to the matter at hand. "Dinner, tonight? I'll text Lily and see if she can come over. We can order food from Ainsley's favorite Chinese place over on Hopkins. Maybe grab a case of beer."

"Chinese food and beer?" I crinkle my nose.

"Good point. Maybe we should play it safe and go with pizza. Oh, and I can stop at the bakery and get her those red velvet cupcakes she loves so much."

"Sounds good to me. Anything I can help with?"

"Nope. Just make sure you're at the house no later than seven."

"Well, considering I don't get off work until then, I'll do my best. But you'll have to forgive me if I'm a few minutes late."

"Yeah, yeah." He shakes his head. "It's not like it's anything formal. Just make sure you're there. The last two years it's just been me and Ainsley. I think she'll appreciate it even more if you and Lily are there, too."

"I wouldn't miss it."

"Perfect. Well, I guess I should get my ass back to work. I'm due to be off at five, but if I don't get this transmission finished I'll be lucky if I get to leave at all." He lifts his chin before turning and walking away.

It's six-thirty when I walk into the house. After telling Jim about Finn's plans for Ainsley, he let me bounce out a little early. But now I'm starting to think that maybe I should have stayed a little longer considering it appears I've beat everyone home.

I know Finn had to go pick everything up, and given that he didn't leave the shop until nearly five-thirty, it shouldn't surprise me that he's not here yet.

Deciding to take a quick shower, I head to my room to grab a change of clothes before I slip into the bathroom. After spending ten minutes under the near scalding water, I emerge feeling like a new man.

Rubbing a towel through my wet hair, I open the door and turn, damn near taking Ainsley out in the process. She runs right into me, clearly not expecting me to step into her path.

Her hands go to my biceps and she squeezes, trying to steady herself. I swear to Christ I can feel the effects of that touch everywhere.

"Shit. Sorry," she fumbles out, looking up to meet my gaze.

"No, I'm sorry. I should have looked before I stepped out." I smile, not able to resist the urge to reach out and sweep a chunk of hair that's fallen into her face away.

When my fingers graze her cheek, her entire expression changes. She blinks once, then twice, tiny puffs of air sliding past her lips.

She's so fucking beautiful I almost lose my mind for a second and pull her closer. Luckily, before I can make what would likely be a colossal mistake, a loud bang sounds through the house.

We quickly break apart, Ainsley turning to head toward the living room with me hot on her trail. When we reach the end of the hallway, we see Finn trying to wiggle his way through the storm door with his hands full.

"What the hell, man." I laugh, taking off toward him. I quickly relieve him of two pizza boxes, waiting until he's inside before closing the door behind him. "You should have called and told me you were here. I would have come out and helped you."

"I thought I could get it all." He laughs. "But then I almost lost the pizza…*Twice*."

"Well, luckily everything still appears to be in one piece."

"What is all this?" Ainsley asks, pulling both of our attention to where she's standing next to the couch.

"Oh shit," he blurts, clearly having not seen her standing there. "Surprise." Finn smiles, holding up the white bakery box. "We're having a little impromptu dinner to celebrate you completing finals and officially being a college senior."

"Finn." She tries to hide her smile but fails miserably. She opens her mouth to say something else, but her attention moves to the front door as someone else enters.

"I brought beer, bitches!" Lily holds up a case of beer in one hand and a fifth of tequila in the other. "Oh, and tequila." She laughs, holding her arms open. "Come give me a hug, senior."

Ainsley shakes her head and then crosses the room, wrapping Lily in a hug.

"You knew about this and didn't tell me?" I hear her say. "I'm pretty impressed. I didn't know you knew how to keep a secret." The two women release each other and Ainsley immediately reaches for the tequila bottle. "But I already told you, no tequila." She turns, shoving the bottle into my chest. "Hide this," she whispers, sliding past me before disappearing into the kitchen.

"Don't even think about it." Lily snags it back out of my hand before I've even thought to move, and quickly follows after Ainsley.

"Women." Finn looks at me and shrugs, laughing as he heads toward the back of the house.

There are two things I've learned tonight.

One, Ainsley is a funny ass drunk who is as light weight as they come. Three beers and three shots in and she can barely keep her words straight.

And two, Finn has a serious thing for her best friend. And if I had to guess, I would say the feeling is mutual. I just haven't figured out if either knows how the other feels or if they're both that oblivious.

Either way, the more they drink, the more their obvious attraction shows through. I know probably better than anyone how Finn behaves when he's trying to impress a girl and let me tell you, he's pulling out all the stops tonight.

While everyone has been throwing back beers and toasting shots, I've spent the last hour nursing my way through two beers. It's not like anyone needs to stay sober for any reason, but I have no desire to get drunk. I just want to sit back and enjoy this feeling. Being home. Being with my family. Things are starting to feel right again. Why would I ever want to drink that away? After being deprived of it for so long, all I want to do is soak it all in and revel in how incredible it all feels.

Eventually, the party moves to the living room where Ainsley gets the bright idea that everyone should play Twister; which ends up being the funniest damn thing I've seen in a very long time. Or maybe ever. Because I'm the only sober one, I'm the only one that has any idea what the hell is going on, which makes the whole thing even more comical.

After several attempts and failures to complete a game, Lily announces she's had enough. And by enough she meant of the game, not the night. Because moments later she has the radio blaring and is pulling Finn into the middle of the living room like it's some glorified dance floor.

Ainsley, either completely clueless as to what's happening between her brother and her best friend or simply not caring, flops down next to me and looks at me with hazy eyes.

"You're really cute." She smiles, a small hiccup bubbling from her throat.

"And you're drunk." I nudge her shoulder with mine.

"Am not," she argues.

"Oh no?" My eyes go down to where her hand settles on the top of my thigh. My groin instantly tightens and I have to fight the urge to guide her hand upward.

Calm the fuck down, Ryland. This is Ainsley…

"Nope." She pops her lips and my gaze goes to her mouth, only further intensifying my arousal.

Feeling like I need to get the fuck out of here for a moment, I quickly stand and head toward the kitchen to grab another beer.

I hear Ainsley following me but I don't turn around to look at her until I have the cap twisted off and a fresh beer pressed to my lips.

"I want to dance," she announces, extending her hand to me.

"What?" I look at her hand and then back up to her face.

"Dance with me." She smiles, wiggling her fingers.

"I know it's been a while, but you know I don't dance."

"Oh come on. It's just us." She gestures around the room at nothing in particular.

"And?"

"And, no one cares if you can't dance."

"I never said I couldn't dance, only that I don't." I chuckle when both of her hands go to her hips and she pouts out her bottom lip the way she always used to do when she was younger. "Don't look at me like that. That only worked when you were little." It's totally working but I'm not going to tell her that.

She promptly drops her hands to her sides, a mischievous grin tugging at the corners of her mouth. She steps toward me and in turn I step back. Not deterred, she takes another step forward, and then another, until she has successfully backed me into the counter.

If I wasn't so worried Finn might walk in at any moment, I might actually be enjoying this little game she's playing.

Ainsley leans in close, her tits pressing into me as she reaches up and locks her hands around the back of my neck. I tense, feeling both uneasy and turned on at the same time.

"So then what does work?" she whispers.

"Ains." I shake my head, trying to put this to a stop as gently as I can. It's not that I don't want her. Fuck, I do. More than I've ever wanted anything before in my entire life. But this is Ainsley. And Ainsley is as off limits as they come.

"Shhh," she slurs, tugging my face down to hers. I know I should resist but for some reason I can't bring myself to stop her. "Do you have any idea how many times I've dreamt of kissing you?" she asks, her fingers tangling in the back of my hair.

With her pressed so tightly against me, her warm breath on my face, I find my will power quickly diminishing by the second. I know if I don't stop this soon, I may not stop it at all.

"I used to lay in bed at night and think about you," she continues. "How I wanted you to be my first kiss. How I wanted you to be my first everything."

The more she talks, the more my head spins.

What is she saying?

"Ainsley," I choke out, needing to just say something to hear myself speak. To remind myself that this is real and not some crazy dream.

"I want you, Ryland. I've always wanted you." She leans in to kiss me, and even though it's the last thing I want to do, I stop her. Grabbing her shoulders, I firmly guide her backward.

Her expression shifts. It goes from sexy and playful to hurt and embarrassed in a matter of seconds and hits me in the gut with such force that it nearly knocks the wind right out of me.

Before I can say anything, she quickly spins around and takes off toward her bedroom.

As much as I want to go after her, I know I shouldn't. Just like as badly as I wanted to kiss her, I knew I couldn't. Not only because she's Finn's little sister but because she's drunk. I'd never forgive myself if I let her do something she would regret, and she probably wouldn't forgive me either.

Maybe what she was saying is true. Maybe she really has harbored some kind of feelings for me. Or maybe she's just drunk. Lord knows I've said some really outlandish things when I've been drinking and more often times than not, there hasn't been an ounce of truth to them.

Then again, Ainsley's never been a bullshitter.

The thought only serves to confuse me further.

Killing the rest of my beer in one long pull, I toss the bottle into the trashcan and head back out to the living room. Finn is stretched out on the couch, some pop shit blaring from the radio, while neither girl is anywhere in sight.

"Where'd everyone go?" I try to act completely natural, like his sister didn't just throw herself at me moments ago in the next room.

"Ainsley wasn't feeling well so Lily went to take care of her." He sits up, swaying slightly as he does.

"Looks like you may want to call it a night." I chuckle.

"Yeah, I think I might." He clamors to his feet. "Would you mind locking up and shutting all this shit off?" He gestures around the room.

"Nah, I got it," I tell him, watching him stumble down the hallway moments later.

"Ryland." Her voice is so soft that for a moment I think I'm dreaming, but then the door opens and a dim yellow light filters in from the hallway. "Are you awake?" I look up to see Ainsley standing in the doorway, her long dark hair hanging around her shoulders.

"I'm awake." I lift my head off the pillow as I watch her enter the room.

Quietly closing the door behind her, the room is once again shrouded in darkness. I hear each step as she takes it and then I feel the bed shift. Moments later she curls into my side, laying her head on my chest in a way she'd done countless times when she was younger.

I don't have the energy to question it as I wrap an arm around her shoulder and pull her in closer.

"I'm sorry about earlier," she whispers, her hand sliding across my stomach before settling on my chest.

"Don't be. You had a lot to drink."

"But I didn't. I mean, not really," she admits quietly. "I knew exactly what I was doing. I still do."

"Ainsley." I attempt to interrupt whatever it is she's planning on saying next, not sure that I want to hear it.

"I know what you're going to say. I'm like a little sister to you and you've never looked at me that way. But that doesn't mean that I haven't wished that you would for most of my life."

"Ains." I slide my hand across her cheek and pull her face upward, her silhouette illuminated by the tiny glimmer of light peaking in from under the door. "It's not like that. When you were younger, yes. But now. Fuck. You have no idea how badly I've wanted to hear everything you were saying tonight. How often I've thought about kissing you since I've been back. How intensely my body craves you. I haven't been able to think of much of anything else since I got out."

"Then do it. Kiss me."

"You have no idea how much I wish I could."

"Why can't you?"

"Because Finn would never forgive me, for one. And two, because I don't trust myself with you. And you shouldn't trust me either."

"I shouldn't. But that doesn't mean that I don't."

"You say that now. Come talk to me tomorrow when you're sober. I doubt you'll feel the same way."

"I *am* sober," she insists, despite the slight slur to her words.

"You may not be puking on yourself drunk, but you're far from sober."

"Don't do that. Don't talk to me like I'm still a child." She tries to sit up but I hold her in place. "My whole life everyone has treated me differently. Like I'm some helpless little girl who can't possibly be capable of taking care of herself or making her own choices. I'm not a little girl. I'm not some delicate flower that needs to be protected. I'm not…"

She never has a chance to finish her sentence because before she can get another word out, I press my lips to hers and for one brief moment I let myself have the one thing I want the most… *Her*.

Chapter 13

Ainsley

I peel my eyes open, one and then the other, as I blink up at the ceiling. Only it's not my ceiling I'm looking at.

Turning my head to the side, my chest swells when I catch sight of Ryland's handsome face as he sleeps soundly next to me.

Memories of last night flood my mind. My drunk confession. Sneaking into his room in the middle of the night. The kiss...

It was everything I had ever dreamed it would be yet so much more at the same time.

One kiss. That's all I got. One kiss and then Ryland tucked me into his side, kissed my forehead, and ordered me to go to sleep.

That's the last thing I remember. Falling asleep in his arms with the taste of him on my lips. And god was it the most perfect night of my life.

It's crazy to think that a week ago I was still harboring some childish grudge against him and now here I am, lying in his bed, feeling more in love with him than I ever have before. Which up until this morning I didn't think was possible.

I'm not foolish enough to believe that this means anything. He made it pretty clear last night that we can't be together. And while the thought darkens my bright mood, it doesn't diminish it completely. Because if last night proves anything, it's that Ryland can be swayed.

I didn't come in here last night expecting for anything to happen. I thought at best I would apologize for my ridiculous behavior and move on. But then as soon as I was laying in his arms, I couldn't stop the word vomit from pouring out.

This is why I don't drink. Because when I do, I have absolutely no filter. Then again, if I hadn't been egged on by liquid courage, I may have missed out on what was hands down the best two minutes of my life.

Even if nothing happens from here, even if that one kiss is all I get, I won't ever be able to bring myself to regret it. Because that one kiss was a lifetime of wishes all rolled into a perfect moment.

As much as I want to lay here and watch Ryland sleep, I know I need to get back to my room. I left Lily sleeping on my floor when I went into Ryland's room, and while I have every intention of telling her what happened, I don't want her to wake up and not be able to find me.

Reluctantly, I lift Ryland's arm, which is draped over my middle, and gently slide out from underneath it. He stirs but doesn't wake and I'm able to roll out of bed without disturbing him.

Tiptoeing across the room, I pull open the door as quietly as I can before stepping out into the hallway, my heartbeat pounding in my ears like a loud bass drum.

I look toward Finn's room, ensuring his door is closed, before stepping out into the hall. I pull Ryland's door shut, breathing out a deep sigh of relief that the whole incident seems to have gone undetected by anyone else in the house.

Reaching for my doorknob, I twist it ever so gently, my attention going to my right before I'm able to get it open. Lily's head pops out of Finn's room, doing a similar move to the one I just pulled, and my eyes damn near bulging out of my head.

When she sees me standing in the hallway, her entire face pales.

What the…

I'm not sure if I'm angry or plain confused to see my best friend sneaking out of my brother's bedroom at the butt crack of dawn.

"I can explain." Her expression turns apologetic as she makes her way toward me.

"Explain?" I question. "Explain what? Why you were in Finn's room?" I whisper hiss at her. "How long has this been going on?" I try to think back over all the times Finn and Lily have been around each other, trying to pinpoint if there's been signs that for whatever reason I seemed to have missed. But I come up blank. If this is something that's been going on before now, either they are really good at lying or I'm blind as a bat.

"What?" She shakes her head at me, reaching around me to push open my bedroom door before shoving me inside.

"Have you two been sleeping together all this time?" I accuse before she can even get the door shut.

"No. Of course not," she insists.

"Then you better start explaining because I'm really freaking confused right now."

Lily takes a deep breath and lets it out slowly, a pink hue crossing her perfect chocolate cheeks. "It just kind of happened."

"Just kind of happened how? You were asleep on my floor at two in the morning. So how did you end up in Finn's room?"

"I woke up and you weren't here. I got up to look for you and ran into Finn as he was coming out of the bathroom. Before I knew what was happening, it was already happening."

"Stop." I hold my hands up. "Stop right there. I don't want to hear another word." I crinkle my nose in disgust. "I seriously cannot right now." I turn, pacing the room. "Lily, you slept with my brother." I throw my arms up, not entirely sure how I feel about this situation.

On one hand, they are both adults and can do whatever the heck they want. On the other, one is my best friend and the other is my brother, which could really complicate things for me in the future should this go sideways.

"I know. God, I'm so sorry, Ains. I mean, you know I've always thought he was a babe. But I never, *ever* thought what happened last night would end up happening. You have to know that."

"I don't know anything right now," I tell her, laughing in spite of myself.

"Please don't be mad at me."

"I'm not mad, Lily. Confused, yes. A little revolted, maybe. Mad, I have no right to be."

"I swear, I never meant for it to happen. But he's just so good looking and oh my god, can he kiss. Lord, I've never had a man kiss me like that."

I instantly hold my hands over my ears and start humming loudly and quite dramatically.

Lily laughs, pulling my hands away.

"Sorry. Your brother. I got it." She smiles. "No more talk of kissing… or other things."

"Lily!" I scold, playfully shoving her shoulder.

Now that the initial shock has worn off, I have to admit, the whole situation is a little bit humorous. Seriously, Lily and Finn. They are so far from two people I would have paired together that it's almost laughable. And yet, it makes total sense at the same time.

"So what, are you two a thing now?" I ask after a brief pause.

"What? No. I mean, I don't think so. We really didn't talk that much." She gives me another apologetic smile.

"Oh god. I think I'm going to be ill." I hold my stomach, clearly messing with her.

"Stop." She giggles, her shoulders relaxing slightly as the tension in the room eases. "Speaking of ending up in someone's room, care to explain to me where you were last night when I went looking for you?"

"The kitchen, I guess." I shrug, plopping down on my bed.

"The kitchen." She gives me a doubtful look.

"Maybe if you had made it past the hallway you would have known that," I challenge, giving her the stink eye.

"Fair enough." She holds her hands up in front of herself. "I wasn't sure. You went to bed so abruptly last night and when I tried to talk to you, you were babbling incoherently about no one wanting you and how you were going to die alone. It was all a little melodramatic."

"Well, how about you remember that the next time you force tequila on me." I point my finger at her.

"I brought it. I didn't force you to drink it."

"You didn't pour it down my throat, I'll give you that. But you sure weren't letting me just say no either. Ever hear of peer pressure."

"Pul-ease. We both know you wouldn't have touched the tequila if you didn't really want to. Ainsley Kenter doesn't let anyone push her into doing something she doesn't want to do."

"Well, I think the least you can do is make me breakfast to make up for it." I smile, honestly surprised I feel even a little hungry after a night of drinking. In fact, I feel really good considering everything.

"Or better yet, how about we go load up on those red velvet cupcakes we didn't eat last night and call it a day."

I think on that for a moment and decide cupcakes sound fantastic right about now.

"Deal." I push up off the bed and practically sprint out of the room, Lily fast on my heels.

We've already managed to demolish a half dozen cupcakes between the two of us when Finn comes strolling into the kitchen a few minutes later. He takes one look at us and shakes his head.

"I don't even want to know," he grumbles, heading straight for the coffee pot.

"No, no you do not." I throw Lily a knowing look. Finn doesn't know that I know what transpired last night. And what kind of sister would I be if I didn't have a little fun with the information. "Lily and I were just discussing this guy she slept with recently. Apparently, he was the worst lay she's ever had," I say, ignoring the shocked look on Lily's face or the way she mouths for me to stop.

I shove another bite of cupcake into my mouth to cover my laughter as Finn's shoulders go rigid as he works to make a pot of coffee.

"She also said he has a tiny peter." I choke out a laugh, garnering me an elbow to the ribs from Lily.

"What the hell did I just walk in on?" Ryland stops in the doorway and the second my gaze lands on him, all humor leaves my body.

I'm instantly transported back to last night. Laying in his bed. His lips moving against mine. The way my body came to life under his touch.

My skin heats just thinking about it.

"Umm." Finn seems extremely uncomfortable as he turns around to face us. "I don't think you want to know," he finishes, the last part of his sentence meant for Ryland.

"Oh no. I definitely think he does," I chime in, refocusing my energy on Lily and Finn rather than obsessing over Ryland. I'll have plenty of time to do that later.

"Know what?" Ryland looks around the room, confusion clear in his expression.

"Apparently, these two had one hell of a night." I gesture between Finn and Lily. "Like a *really* good night, if you know what I mean." I wink dramatically.

"For fuck's sake, Ainsley," Finn groans. "So what was all that shit just now? You were purposely fucking with me?"

"Maybe." I shrug innocently, shoving another large bite of cupcake into my mouth.

"Fucking little sisters, man," he grumbles to Ryland before turning back to the coffee pot. I meet Ryland's gaze and throw him a cupcake filled smile. He rewards me with his own smile and it makes me feel like melting into a puddle all over the floor.

Clearly he feels good about last night as well. Or at least that's what his actions and mood would suggest. The thought makes my already good mood soar.

"So, you and Lily?" Ryland says as he steps up next to Finn.

Lily drops her face into her hands, clearly not finding this as amusing as I am.

"You guys, I'm sitting right here," she announces when Ryland goes as far as to ask Finn how she was in bed.

"Awe, Lil, we're just messing with you." I wrap my arm around her shoulder and give her a squeeze. "No one thinks any less of you for sleeping with my brother," I tell her, laughing when she shoves me off of her.

"What has gotten into you today?" She cocks a brow at me.

"What do you mean?" I can't wipe the smile from my face.

"Exactly what it sounds like. First you're mad, then you're laughing, now you're poking fun at me like this is all a big joke. Are you sure you're feeling okay?" She holds the back of her hand up to my forehead.

"I feel great," I tell her, pushing her hand away.

"Maybe a little too great," she murmurs under her breath so only I can hear.

This seems to get the reaction she wants and her gaze instantly shoots to Ryland before coming back to me, a million questions in her eyes.

"Perhaps I'm not the only one that did something unexpected last night," she whispers.

I immediately shake my head and hold a finger to my lips.

"I wish it was what you were thinking," I mouth, just as surprised as she is by my confession.

"What are you two whispering about over there?" Finn interrupts our hushed conversation.

"Oh nothing. Lily's just telling me more about what a disappointment you were," I fire at Finn, garnering me another elbow from Lily.

"Ainsley!" she objects, her gaze swinging to Finn. "I swear I didn't say that."

"Well, this isn't an awkward morning after or anything," Ryland observes, sliding down into the chair to my right, holding a steaming cup of coffee in his hands. "And here I thought nothing could top Carol Baxter."

"Seriously, Ryland, not you, too." Finn throws Lily an apologetic glance as he takes the seat between her and Ryland.

"Who's Carol Baxter?" I grin, enjoying this way more than I should be.

"No one," Finn cuts Ryland off before he can say anymore.

Ryland chuckles, clearly as amused as I am.

"Why don't you two fuck off and give me and Lily a chance to talk?" he suggests.

"You don't have to ask me twice." Ryland stands, glancing down at me. "You coming, Ains?"

"Right behind you." I climb to my feet and quickly follow him out of the kitchen and into the living room.

He settles down on one side of the couch while I claim the other, clicking on the morning news before pulling my legs up underneath me.

"So Lily and Finn, huh?" he says after a couple minutes of silence have stretched between us. "I don't know about you, but I totally saw that one coming."

"You did?" My surprised expression swings in his direction.

"You didn't?" He quirks a brow at me. "How could you miss it? The way they were all over each other last night."

"I guess I was a little preoccupied with other things."

"Speaking of other things." He lowers his voice. "About last night."

I hold my hand up to stop him.

"I already know what you're going to say, so don't. I won't say anything to Finn. We can chalk it up to Ainsley drinking too much. And as far as everyone is concerned, it never happened."

"Just like that?" He takes a tentative sip of his coffee, watching me over the rim of his cup.

"Just like that." I nod, looking back at the television.

"Ains." His soft voice coaxes my gaze back to him. "I don't want to pretend like it didn't happen."

It's all he's able to say before Finn and Lily come strolling into the room. Lily slides down between me and Ryland while Finn takes the chair.

My stomach is a ball of nerves and all I want to do is drag Ryland out of this room and ask him what he meant by that. But knowing I can do no such thing, I turn my attention to Lily.

"All good?" I ask, smiling at my best friend.

"All good," she confirms with a smile so wide it nearly splits her face in half.

I look over at my brother who's watching us with a grin on his face as well.

"I asked Lily to have dinner with me tonight. And she said yes. You got a problem with that?"

I slide my hand in front of my mouth to cover my smile. "Nope, no problem at all." I giggle.

"Good." He nods once, turning his attention to the television as if to say, 'that's the end of that.'

I'm not sure what the hell was in the air last night, but clearly a lot of shit went down. For starters, I kissed the man I've been dreaming of kissing since I was old enough to know what kissing was. And now, suddenly, my best friend and older brother are dating?

I feel like I'm suffering from a case of wicked whiplash. It's like I woke up yesterday and everything was one way, then I woke up today and everything was completely upside down.

I glance over at Ryland who just so happens to look over at me at the exact same moment. Our eyes lock and something unspoken passes between us. Something that causes my palms to sweat and the little hairs on the back of my neck to stand. Something that makes me extremely nervous and yet equally excited. And I have no idea what it is.

I blink, finally breaking the moment. When I look over at Finn, I find him watching me, a curious look on his face. I smile in an attempt to seem completely natural but I'm not sure if he buys it. Then again, maybe I'm just extremely paranoid.

Besides, what right does he have to say anything? I caught *my* best friend sneaking out of *his* bedroom.

At the same time, I know this is different. Even if I don't want it to be.

Chapter 14

Ainsley

"All ready for your date?" I stop in the hallway when I catch sight of Finn primping his hair in the bathroom.

"Just about." He wipes his hands on the towel in front of him and turns to face me. "How do I look?" He holds out his arms.

"You look good," I admit, taking in his dark jeans and short sleeve gray button down. "Though I have to say, I don't think I've ever seen you so dressed up before."

"Too dressed up?" he questions.

"No, no. I think you look perfect. It's just… different, is all."

"Listen, I know this is sudden and we kind of caught you off guard this morning…"

"Kind of?" I snort out.

"Okay, we really caught you off guard. But the truth is, Ains, I've had a huge crush on Lily for a while and I've kept my distance for your sake. Last night things changed and I really hope you can get on board with the two of us feeling this thing out because I really like her."

"I can see that. And don't worry about me. I love Lily and I love you. As long as you two don't end up hating each other or making it extremely awkward for me, then I'm good with whatever."

"Thanks, Ains." He steps into the hallway with me, dropping an arm over my shoulder as he leads us into the living room. "You going to be okay with it being just you and Ryland tonight?"

"Of course. Nothing we haven't done a million times before." I blow it off like it's nothing, when in reality I've been dying to get him alone all day so I can figure out what his comment this morning meant.

The thought of possibly kissing him again sends a thrill through me so intense that I have trouble keeping a straight face.

"I know, but things are still on shaky ground with you two. I don't want you to feel like I'm throwing you to the wolves."

I laugh. "Seriously, Finn. We'll be fine," I tell him, grabbing his car keys off the coffee table before shoving them in his hand. "Now get out of here or you're going to be late." I usher him toward the door.

"Wait." He stops, looking around the room as he pats his pockets. "Wallet. Phone. Keys." He nods. "I think I have everything."

"I don't think I've ever seen you this nervous about a date before," I point out.

"I don't think I've ever been this nervous for a date before. Lily is…" He pauses. "Different. Special."

"Yes, she is," I agree. "And don't you forget it." I step around him and open the door. "Now go."

Finn takes a deep breath and quickly blows it out, turning to drop a kiss on the top of my head.

"Thanks, Ains," he murmurs.

"Yeah. Yeah. You two have fun." I stand in the open doorway until Finn has pulled out of the driveway. Stepping inside, I close the door and slide the deadbolt in place.

"He gone?" I jump at the sound of Ryland's voice.

"Shit, you scared me," I tell him, turning to see him leaning in the doorway of the hallway where it opens up to the living room.

"Sorry. I didn't want to interrupt whatever you two were talking about."

"We weren't talking about anything. Not really. He just left for his date with Lily." I hitch my thumb back toward the door.

"And how do you feel about that? Your brother dating your best friend?"

"It's totally fine." I shrug, plopping down on the couch moments later.

"Ainsley, it's me. You can tell me how you're really feeling." He chuckles, pushing away from the wall. "I know a lot has changed over the last five years, but I hope you know you can still talk to me about anything."

"I know." I flip on the television, feeling more awkward than I think I ever have when alone with Ryland. When I was younger nothing felt more comfortable to me.

"Okay," he draws out, taking the seat at the opposite end of the couch so that we're both sitting in the exact same spots as this morning.

I chew on the inside of my cheek as I mull over his original question.

"It's weird," I finally admit.

"What's weird?" He cocks a brow; his mind having already moved on.

"Lily and Finn," I admit. "It's weird. Don't you think?" I pull my leg up as I angle my body in his direction.

"Not really. Then again, I don't really know Lily. To me, she's just a girl Finn is interested in. But clearly it's weird for you."

"No, it isn't. Okay, maybe a little." I laugh, shaking my head. "It's just, well, what if it doesn't work out and they end up hating each other?"

"I guess that's a risk you take with any relationship. You can't base your life on what ifs.

You have to embrace the good stuff when it comes along and hope for the best."

"Yeah, I guess." I blow out a breath.

"Look at it this way, maybe they'll end up getting married and spending the rest of their lives happy and in love. I'm sure you'd love that for both of them."

"Of course I would."

"See. There's always the worry that something will go wrong. We don't stop often enough to ask ourselves what would happen *if* it goes right."

"What did they do to you in prison?" I pull my other leg up and shift further inward, resting my back against the arm rest of the couch. "I don't remember you being so… insightful."

"When you're staring at the same four walls day in and day out for over five years, all there is to do is think. I guess it forced me to look at things differently than I used to."

"What was it like? Being in there."

"Lonely." A sad smile tugs at his lips. "You're surrounded by people almost all the time, yet I've never felt more alone than I did while I was there."

"I'm sorry."

"Don't be. I would do it all over again if I had to."

The comment seems weird to me, but for whatever reason, I choose not to question what he means by it.

"I should have come to visit you," I say instead, my voice soft.

"I'm glad you didn't." He catches my hurt expression and quickly moves to explain. "I never wanted you anywhere near that place."

"It was that bad?"

"Yes." He nods. "And no. Just like everything else, when you do something for so long it starts to become your new normal. Eventually I got used to the routine, the people, the lifestyle. But it's not a world I would ever want you to have any part of."

"Is it weird being out?"

"The first few days were a little rough. Even now I can't say I've fully adjusted to being out, but it's getting better. I still go to bed every night convinced I'm going to wake up and be back in that cell and all of this was a dream. When you're on the inside there's a part of you that feels like you'll never get out."

"That must have been so hard for you." I knot my hands in my lap. "I was so angry at you for so long that I never really stopped to think about what you must have been going through. Honestly, I think it was easier for me to pretend that you left on your own free will. It was easier to be mad at you for what you did than to focus on why I was really so hurt."

"Ainsley."

"It's okay." I offer a soft smile. "I was fifteen. I wasn't emotionally equipped to deal with you being gone or why you were gone for that matter. After my mom and dad, I thought you of all people would always be there. And then suddenly you weren't."

"I never wanted to hurt you." He turns toward me, throwing his arm over the back of the couch. "That's the last thing I ever wanted."

"I know that now. At the time I was just so angry. I was mad at you, at Finn, at the entire world."

"What you said last night…" He swallows, his Adam's apple bobbing as he does.

"I meant it," I admit, knowing there's no point in back pedaling. Truthfully I don't want to take it back. Even though Ryland now knowing how I felt, how I *feel*, is embarrassing, it's also freeing. "I've been secretly in love with you for a very long time." I laugh lightly, trying to lighten the admission.

"How long is a very long time?"

"Since I was twelve, maybe."

"Twelve." He chokes over the word. "I had no idea."

"How could you have? It's not like there was a blaring neon sign on my forehead or anything. Besides, I probably would have died if you had found out."

"And yet you're telling me now."

"I'm not a kid anymore."

"That you most certainly are not." His eyes do a quick sweep over my face.

"I'm sorry about last night." I pause and then, "You know what, no, I'm not. I may have said it after drinking too much, but it didn't make it any less true. I'm glad you know. I'm glad you can see why I was so mad at you for so long."

"Ainsley."

"Don't. I already know what you're going to say." I hold my hand up to stop him.

"Actually, I don't think you do." He shifts toward me, not stopping until less than a foot separates us. "I may not have felt the way you did all those years ago, but that doesn't mean things haven't changed. I told you last night, you're all I've been able to think about. That wasn't a lie."

My heart kicks up speed, pounding so rapidly against my ribs that the impact vibrates through my entire body.

"But you also said we can't," I remind him, my voice barely above a whisper.

"We can't," he confirms. "Or at least we shouldn't. But that doesn't mean I don't want to.

Fuck, Ainsley, it's all I want. Kissing you last night, holding you, I should regret it, or at the very least feel guilty, but I don't. I don't feel any of those things because all I can think about is doing it again."

"Me, too," I whisper.

He takes a deep breath in and slowly blows it out through his nose like he's trying to reel himself in, but isn't sure if he can. I know the feeling all too well right about now.

He's not the only one that feels conflicted. But unlike him, I've spent my entire life denying myself the things I really want. Well, not anymore.

Shifting up onto my knees, I throw my leg over his before settling onto his lap.

"We can't," he reiterates when my fingers slide into the back of his hair.

"We can." I lean forward so our faces are so close our noses nearly touch. "I know you're worried about Finn. So am I. But I've spent my entire life denying myself of the thing I've wanted the most out of fear of rejection or what my brother would think. But now here you are, sitting in front of me, telling me that you want me. How could I possibly ignore that and go back to pretending like my feelings aren't real?"

"He would never forgive me," he whispers.

"He doesn't have to forgive what he doesn't know." I tangle my fingers around the ends of his hair and tug his face upward slightly.

"What are you suggesting right now, Ains?" His voice is hoarse, his expression tense.

"That we see what this is. Just you and me. If it doesn't work then no one has to be the wiser. But what if it does? What were you saying earlier about even though it could turn out bad, it can also turn out good?"

"Using my words against me, I see." A grin tugs at his mouth.

"Do you want me?" I shift on his lap, my hands sliding to cup his face.

"I do." His gaze drops to my lips before darting back to my eyes.

"Then that's good enough for me."

Without giving him a chance to object, I press my lips against his. It starts out slow, tentative, but it doesn't stay that way for long. I've spent half my life dreaming about what it would feel like to kiss Ryland Thorpe, and let me tell you, it's a million times better than I ever imagined.

I didn't realize how much he was holding back last night, how hesitant the kiss had been, until now. It's like suddenly there's no barrier between us. It's not about our friendship. It's not about my brother. It's not about our past. It's about right now. It's about him and me. It's about all the things I've felt and never been able to express.

It's about the way it feels to be pressed against him so intimately. The way his hands roam my back. The way soft groans vibrate from his lips as I grind down on his arousal. It's all of it. It's Ryland. It's me. It's *us*.

"Ainsley," Ryland breathes against my mouth.

"I'm not stopping," I tell him, sliding my tongue against his.

I've never been this person. Forward, demanding, unapologetic about what I want. Maybe it's Ryland and the effect he has on me. Or maybe it's me, not willing to give him up now that I know what this feels like.

"We have to." His hands close around my biceps and he forces me backward, breaking the kiss. "We have to stop." His breathing is erratic and the look in his eyes tells me that stopping is the last thing he wants to do.

"Why?" I ask, disappointment seeping into my chest.

"Because I don't want to hurt you."

"You're hurting me by pushing me away."

"I'll be hurting you even more if I let you rush into this and you end up regretting it."

I pull back further and hit him with an exasperated expression.

"Have you not been listening to anything I've said? I want you. I've wanted you over half my life. I'm not going to regret a single moment of being with you."

"You say that now." His expression softens. "But it's easy to throw caution to the wind in the heat of the moment."

"For fuck's sake." I rock back onto his knees, throwing my hands up in frustration. "When are you going to stop this?"

"Stop what?" He seems confused.

"This." I gesture between us. "You're always trying to protect me."

"I'm never going to stop trying to protect you."

"I'm not a little girl anymore. And it's not like I've never had sex." I don't miss the way he flinches at my words. I hadn't even considered that learning I'm not a virgin would be hard for him to hear but given his reaction, it certainly was. "It's not like you're going to rob me of my virtue or anything."

"Jesus, Ainsley. Who are you?" He looks slightly dumbfounded.

"I'm still me. I'm just not the me you remember. I'm all grown up now."

"I know you are." He sighs.

"Then let me make my own choices."

"Ains." He seems so conflicted that I almost feel bad for him.

"I'm serious, Ryland. Either you want me or you don't. Either you're in with me or you're not."

"I'm here, aren't I?"

"And yet you're still fighting it. Forget about Finn. Forget about me and who I am to you. Look at me like you would any other woman."

"But you're not just any other woman, Ainsley."

"Yes I am," I insist. "I am. And I want you to treat me that way. Treat me like I'm some girl you just met and brought home. Don't worry about how it's going to make me feel or if I'm going to regret it."

"But I am worried."

"Please." I lean forward again, sliding my hands around the back of his neck as I drop my forehead to his. "Please, for this one night, let me be the woman you want and not your best friend's little sister."

"But what if you're both?"

"I don't want to be both. I don't want my brother or anyone else to have anything to do with this. I want you to look at me and only see what's in front of you. I want you to see me."

"I do see you." My skin heats as his hands slide underneath the back of my shirt.

"Prove it." I drop my mouth and press a kiss to his lips. "I'm not some delicate piece of glass you're going to break." I slide my tongue along the seam of his lips. "I want this. I want *you*."

"Fuck." He lets out an almost painful groan before his hand is in my hair and his mouth crashes over mine, kissing me so forcefully it would probably hurt if it didn't feel so damn good.

He shifts with me still in his lap and pushes to his feet, taking me along with him like I weigh nothing.

His hands are everywhere. My hair. My back. My ass. Everywhere he can reach as he carries me to my bedroom.

It isn't until I'm lying on top of my bed, watching him slide his shirt over his head, that the magnitude of what's about to happen sets in.

He pops open the button of his jeans, his gray eyes taking me in as he slowly slides them down his hips and peels them off his legs.

I can't look away.

Hell, I can't even breathe.

Everything I've ever dreamt of is happening. It's happening and yet I'm so nervous and wired with anticipation that I'm not sure I'm fully soaking in a single moment of it.

As much effort as it took for me to get him here, I expected it to be different. I expected him to continue to handle me with kid gloves and be overly gentle. But boy was I wrong.

He's demanding and rough. Stripping me out of my clothes in a matter of seconds. He kisses my body, nips and sucks so hard I know there will be marks. His fingers dig into my hips as he slides me to the edge of the bed, and when he pulls one of my nipples into his mouth and bites down, I'm not sure if the scream that rips from my throat is one of pain or pleasure, or maybe both.

I love it.

I love every single second of it.

Because it's what I asked for.

Right now I'm not Ainsley, Finn's little sister.

Right now I am a woman and he is a man. And together we are taking everything that we want with no real thought of consequence or what happens next. Truthfully, none of that matters.

And when Ryland finally settles between my thighs, his condom covered erection nudging at my entrance, I feel so drunk with lust that I can't see anything but what's directly in front of me… *Him*.

I buck upward as Ryland slides inside of me. I swear, the instant the contact is made, I've never felt more alive. Something awakens inside of me. Something I don't think I ever knew existed. Like an untamed animal that only knows how to survive on instinct, I become unhinged.

I scratch and claw. I bite and scream. I become a completely different person under the blinding pleasure coursing through me.

I've never felt anything like it before and I never want to feel anything but it for the rest of my life.

I want it deeper, harder, faster. I want everything he can give and more. And that he does.

He takes me from the top, he takes me from behind, at one point he even picks me up and pins me to the wall. We are like two super cells coming together to create the ultimate storm, one that no one will survive.

Together we go up and then back down, pulling every ounce of pleasure we can from each other.

It's unlike anything I ever thought two people could share. It's unlike anything I ever thought I would experience in my life. And yet it's exactly like I knew it would be.

Ryland and I have always had a special connection, one that ran deeper than any I've shared with anyone else. He's been the driving force behind every decision I've ever made. Whether I've been willing to admit it or not.

And when he collapses down on top of me, his body spent, his lungs begging for air, his heart thrumming wildly against my chest, I know with complete certainty what I want for the rest of my life.

I want him.

I always have. I know I always will.

Because now he doesn't just own my heart.

He owns my body as well…

Chapter 15

Ryland

I should feel guilty. Looking down at Ainsley half asleep in my arms, I should feel something. Some sense of remorse. Only I don't. I can't bring myself to feel the slightest ounce of regret. How can I, when right now, for the first time maybe in my entire life, everything feels perfect. Like this is how it was always meant to be.

I'm sated and spent in the best fucking way possible

Being with Ainsley was like having an out of body experience. I knew what was happening. My body could feel every touch, every quiver of her beneath me. I could hear every moan and whimper. But at the same time I felt like I was outside of my body, watching it all.

It was the strangest sensation. Yet, hands down the most incredible sexual experience of my life. And truthfully that's really saying something considering I've slept with more than my fair share of women over the years.

And it's not because it's been five years since I was with a woman. I think it would have felt the same if I had just had sex yesterday. Because it wasn't about the physical act of having sex. It was about who I was having sex with.

A sound startles me out of my sleepy haze and I jump. Ainsley flies into a sitting position and hits me with a bewildered expression.

"Shit. He's not home already, is he?" Her mind seems to go in the exact same direction as mine.

"I wouldn't think so." I glance at the clock. Finn and Lily have only been gone a couple of hours. I expected them to be out much later than this.

"I'll go check." Ainsley throws back the covers and rolls out of bed before I can even think to stop her. "If he's home this early then Lily is probably with him." She quickly slides on her shorts and bra, scouring the floor for her tank top. I take a moment to study her curves. Her slender stomach, her ample chest, her cute little belly button that's still an outie, even though when she was little she insisted it would eventually dip in like most everyone else's does. She always hated that hers stuck out. "Unless it went horribly and then maybe not," she adds, locating her shirt before tossing it on.

"Wait," I hiss as she reaches the door. "What if he realizes I'm in here?"

"Who cares if he does?" She shrugs. "I'll tell him we were talking. He won't suspect a thing unless we give him a reason to."

I guess she's not wrong there. Finn knows how close Ainsley and I used to be. It was nothing for me to be alone with her in her room often. Hell, I used to sleep on her floor all the time when she was a kid and he never thought a thing of it. And rightfully so. I never would have crossed that line with his sister. Especially given how young she was at the time. And while yes, thirteen or fourteen isn't horribly young, it was young enough that I never would have even entertained the idea. But now? Well, Ainsley isn't that little girl anymore and a man can only resist so much.

"I'm coming with you," I tell her, reluctantly rolling out of bed. I snag my boxers off the floor as I hear the door open.

My heart just about leaps out of my fucking chest at the sound, but then I look up and realize Ainsley is the one who opened the door.

"Just stay here. It'll look more suspicious if both of us come clamoring out at the same time." She slips into the hallway and pulls the door closed behind her before I've even managed to get my boxers halfway on.

Deciding that I should probably get dressed either way, I quickly locate the rest of my clothing.

I'm just buckling my jeans when Ainsley re-enters the room.

"No one's here." She holds her hands up like she has no idea where the noise we heard came from.

"You're sure? It sounded like it came from inside the house."

"I'm sure. But by all means, feel free to go check it out if you don't believe me."

"I believe you. But I'll feel better if I look around just to be sure."

"Be my guest." She pushes the bedroom door the rest of the way open and gestures to the dimly lit hall. "While you do that, I'm going to make myself a sandwich. You want one?"

"That depends, what kind of sandwich are you making?" I give her a knowing look.

"Peanut butter and banana, of course." She smiles.

"So that's still a thing of yours, huh?" I chuckle. When Ainsley was little, peanut butter and banana sandwiches were one of the only things Finn and their dad could get her to eat. I don't know why, but it gives me some comfort knowing that there's still little parts of the girl I knew in there.

"Always. Though I've now taken to sprinkling cinnamon on top. It elevates it to a whole other level. You have to try it."

"You're really fucking cute, you know that?" I can't resist the urge to say.

"I'm cute?" She crinkles her nose.

"What? Cute is a good thing."

"Cute is what you call a kitten or a child."

"Then what would you prefer I call you?"

"I don't know. Whatever you want. Sexy. Irresistible. Drop dead gorgeous." She hesitates when I step up in front of her. "You take your pick." She fakes indifference.

"How about, all of the above?" I slide an arm around her waist and tug her toward me.

It still feels crazy as fuck to look down and see that it's Ainsley in my arms. Ainsley, the girl that used to make me walk around the house with her little body wrapped around my leg. Little Ainsley. My Ainsley.

Well, I guess some things haven't changed. Because *mine* is exactly what she is. After touching her, tasting her, feeling her come undone beneath me, there's no way I'm ever giving her up.

I lean down and brush my lips against hers, my groin stirring when she whimpers against my mouth.

"Sexy." I slide my nose against hers. "Irresistible." I nip at her jawline. "Drop dead gorgeous." I kiss the side of her neck. "How's that?" I pull back, not able to hide my smile.

"Not bad." She presses up on her tip toes and kisses my cheek. "But your delivery could use some work." With that, she spins around and takes off down the hallway, leaving me with her laughter floating around me.

I have half a mind to chase after her, but wanting to make sure Finn isn't home first, I head to his room, knocking before pushing the door open. The lights are off and there's no one inside. Pulling the door shut, I check the bathroom next, not bothering to check my room as I know he wouldn't go in there, before heading out into the living room. Everything appears to be quiet and there's no sign of Finn.

Once I'm satisfied that we are still alone, I head toward the kitchen. I find Ainsley standing at the counter with her back to me, a butter knife covered in peanut butter in one hand and a piece of bread in the other. She glances back at me when she hears me enter.

"You didn't actually say if you wanted one or not, but I'm making you one anyway." She leans into me when I slide up next to her.

"Good, because I'm famished." I chuckle, dropping a kiss to the side of her head.

"Will you…" Her words die in her throat when the sound of glass breaking echoes through the house. "What was that?" she whispers, her eyes wide with fear.

"I'm not sure. Stay here. Let me go check it out."

"No wait." She drops the butter knife and bread onto the plate before grabbing my arm. "Don't leave me in here alone."

"Okay, but stay behind me," I tell her, holding an arm behind me so that she can hold onto me as we make our way through the house.

Like the first pass I made, everything seems normal. The doors are locked and nothing seems out of place. When we reach the end of the hall, I peer into Ainsley's open door. The light is still on and everything seems fine.

Turning, I hold a finger to my mouth before releasing Ainsley's hand and stepping into the room. I do a quick scan to make sure no one is inside before gesturing for her to follow me.

"Ryland." I freeze at the sound of Ainsley's voice, turning to see her gaze locked on her dresser. "My drawers are open," she whispers.

"They weren't open before?"

"No."

"You're sure?"

"Positive."

"Don't move," I instruct, getting on the floor to check under her bed.

"Check the closet," she says, her arms wrapped nervously around herself.

I cross the room and peer inside the small closet. If someone was hiding in here I'd know it instantly because of how tiny the space is.

"Nothing." I turn back toward her. "We've already checked everywhere." I realize as I finish the sentence that's not actually true. "Shit," I grumble, quickly stepping past Ainsley back into the hallway.

"Ryland," she hisses, following so close behind me that she runs into me when I slow to a stop in front of my bedroom door.

Slowly turning the knob, I throw it open fast so that if anyone is inside they won't have time to hide. Flipping on the light, it takes me less than a second to realize where the glass breaking noise came from. The lamp that normally sits on my bedside table is now on the floor and there are broken pieces of the glass base scattered over the worn hardwood.

I feel Ainsley tense as she steps up next to me and my gaze swings to her.

"The window." She points, drawing my attention to the back wall where the window is wide open, the curtains blowing in the light breeze coming in from outside.

Doing a quick sweep of the room, I check under the bed and in the closet just as I did with Ainsley's room, before finally assessing the window situation.

Upon initial inspection it looks like someone may have entered and exited the house through my bedroom window, likely knocking over the lamp on their way back out. But other than the broken lamp, nothing in my room seems out of place. In fact, my wallet is still sitting on top of the dresser untouched. Which leads me to believe that whoever came here didn't come here to rob the place.

My insides instantly tighten at the thought.

Shoving the window closed, I click the lock in place before turning back toward Ainsley.

"Do you have any idea who would want to break into your house or why?"

"No." She shakes her head adamantly.

"Let's do another full sweep of the house and make sure that whoever it was is gone."

"Okay, but I'm staying with you," she tells me, like I would let her leave my sight for even one second knowing that someone could still be inside.

I nod, pulling her back out into the hallway with me.

After thoroughly inspecting the house, Ainsley and I both come to the same conclusion. Whoever was here either had no intention of robbing the place or they got spooked when they realized someone was home and took off before they got the chance.

"They must have come in here after we went out to the kitchen," Ainsley says, clinging tightly to me as we make our way back into her bedroom.

Once we're both inside, she turns, closing and locking the door.

"But why would they do that? They had to have known shortly after they entered the house that someone was here. So why risk coming into your room and rummaging through drawers?" I ask, something about this entire thing not sitting right with me.

"I don't know," she murmurs, making her way toward the dresser. She looks inside the two top drawers for a long moment before turning back to me, a horrified look on her face.

"What? What is it?"

"They stole some of my underwear." Her voice is so soft I almost can't make out the words.

"They what?" I question anyway.

"They stole some of my underwear," she repeats a little louder this time.

"Are you sure?" I quickly cross the room toward her.

"I'm positive." She points inside the small drawer on the left. "I just did laundry earlier this afternoon." She clears her throat. "Why would someone break into my house and only take those items?"

"I can think of a few reasons," I grind out, anger bubbling in my chest. "This is my fault."

"What?" She draws back. "How is any of this your fault?"

"Because I left the bedroom window unlocked. I know what kind of sick fucks hang around this neighborhood."

"You didn't leave the window unlocked. The lock is broken. Even if you lock it, it doesn't actually lock. Besides, I leave my window open all the time when the weather's nice. Not to mention our front door is unlocked more often than not."

"That doesn't make me feel any better." I turn, pacing to the other side of the room.

"What I don't understand, though," she says, thinking aloud. "Is how someone would know where to go unless they had been here before?"

"What do you mean?" I stop moving, my gaze locking with hers across the room.

"Think about it. They came in through your bedroom, my dad's old room. Pretty much anyone who's ever been here knows that room is usually unoccupied. And it just so happens to have a window that doesn't lock, which makes it the perfect place to sneak in undetected. Then, add on the fact that whoever it was obviously knew what they were looking for and where to look. If it wasn't for them knocking the lamp over on their way out we probably would never have even known they were here."

"So you think it was someone you know?" I question, knowing that out of the two scenarios, this would likely be the worst case. When it's someone you know, it makes it that much more personal.

"Maybe." She chews on her lower lip as she mulls it over. "God, I don't know. Maybe I'm just trying to make sense of it. I know it's only some underwear, but knowing someone came in here and stole something of mine, something so intimate and private, it really creeps me out."

"You have every reason to feel that way." I cross the room toward her, tugging her into my arms. "I'm so sorry this happened."

"So am I. And not because of some stupid underwear but because what started out as probably the best night of my life is now being overshadowed by some douche bag breaking into my house."

"The best night of your life?" I pull back slightly, smiling down at her.

"I said *probably*," she fires back, purposely trying to burst my bubble.

"For what it's worth, it would take a hell of a lot more than someone breaking in to diminish how this evening began." I tip her chin upward.

"Is that so?" She relaxes slightly in my arms.

"It is. And…" I lean down and kiss her mouth. "If we hurry, maybe we can end on just as high of a note." I slide my tongue along the seam of her lips.

"You're trying to distract me." *How well she knows me.*

"Is it working?" I smile against her mouth.

"Maybe," she admits, wrapping her arms around the back of my neck.

"Maybe?" I chuckle. "Maybe I should stop then." I start to pull away but her grip on me instantly tightens, holding me in place.

"Don't you dare," she warns, angling her head just in time for me to slide my tongue against hers. She whimpers into my mouth and I swear I nearly come undone still fully clothed.

What have I gotten myself into?

Chapter 16

Ainsley

"Wait." Lily holds her hands up. "You mean to tell me not only did your house get broken into, but you also slept with Ryland last night?" She gapes at me. When she came home with Finn, we'd told them about the break in, but that was where we'd stopped sharing the events of the evening. "And you're just telling me this now?" She doesn't try to hide the hurt that slides across her pretty face.

"It's not like it happened a week ago. It was yesterday. And truthfully, I needed some time to process everything before I said it out loud. Besides, when was I supposed to tell you? When you were standing next to my brother?" I give her a knowing look.

"Fair enough," she admits. "So, you slept with Ryland." She shakes her head. "You slept with Ryland." It's like she's trying to wrap her head around it.

"How many times are you going to say it?"

"As many times as I have to. I'm processing here."

"Listen, I know you and Finn are doing this whole dating thing now," I say, still not entirely sure how I feel about them seeing each other. "But you cannot say a word to him. He would kill Ryland…and me."

"Is that why you didn't tell me right away? Because you thought I would tell Finn?" She leans back away from the table, her water glass clenched in between both hands.

"What? Of course not." I immediately deny the accusation even though deep down it definitely weighed on my decision when I was trying to decide whether to tell her at all.

A part of me wanted to keep it between me and Ryland, but then I realized that not having anyone to talk to about it was killing me, which is why I invited Lily out for Mexican. I needed a safe space where I could talk freely and not have to worry about being overheard.

It wasn't until this morning that I realized just how paper thin the walls in our house are. Finn and Ryland were talking in Ryland's bedroom as they were fixing the lock on his window and I could hear everything they said. I swear it sounded like they were standing right in front of me.

I hadn't considered the fact that our rooms share a wall or what that might mean as far as being able to hear things from the other rooms. No one has lived in there since my dad passed away eight years ago so I never noticed. Of course, that caused me to reevaluate every conversation I've had in my room since Ryland moved in and I'd be lying if I said I wasn't a little panicked over what he may have heard.

"I know this thing between me and Finn is sudden but I'm still your best friend. I would never betray your trust that way. I hope you know that."

"I do. Of course I do. I just wasn't sure what to say at the time. Hell, I'm still not. It just kind of happened."

"Things don't just kind of happen. Something always starts them." She arches a perfectly shaped eyebrow at me. "It was the night before last, wasn't it?

"Oh, you mean the night you snuck off and boned my brother?" I can't stop myself from saying.

"One, who says bone anymore?" She snorts. "And two, I thought you were okay with me and Finn."

"I am," I insist, wishing I could take back the snarky comment. It's clear that Lily is worried about the effect this is going to have on our relationship, and as her friend I really shouldn't give her more grief than necessary. "And yes, it was the same night," I tack on, hoping to propel the conversation forward because right now I really need to hash this whole Ryland thing out with my best friend.

"I knew something went down but you never told me what."

"Probably because you were too busy with my brother." I can't stop myself. "Sorry." I don't know what is wrong with me right now.

"Ainsley, if you're not okay with me and Finn, you need to tell me now. Don't play this passive aggressive game with me where you pretend like everything is fine when it isn't."

"I am okay with it. I really am," I insist. "I'm just having a bit of a mental meltdown here."

"Then stop with the snark and talk to me."

"I'm sorry." I blow out a breath. "It wouldn't be so bad had Ryland initiated this whole thing, but he didn't, I did. And now I'm second guessing myself. He barely spoke to me today. I'm starting to freak out a little."

"Well, have you stopped to think about why this might be?"

"What do you mean?"

"I mean, has he even had the opportunity to talk to you? Finn was home all day was he not?"

"Yeah." I stab a fork into my taco salad.

"Ryland probably doesn't want to raise any suspicion so he's keeping his distance around Finn. Finn thinks you two are still on shaky ground. Acting like you are best friends all of a sudden might raise some red flags."

"Hmm. I hadn't really thought of that," I admit. "I just thought maybe Ryland was having second thoughts."

"Given the way he kept looking at you the other night, I don't think that's the case."

"What do you mean?" My heartrate spikes.

"I'm just saying, that man looks at you like the sun rises and sets with you. If he's keeping his distance, it's not because he's lost interest or is having second thoughts, of that much I'm sure."

"You don't even know him. How can you be so sure?"

"I may not know *him* well but I know men. Just trust me on this one, girl."

"I wish I shared your confidence. I just feel so all over the place. It's like one minute I'm pissed that he's back and the next I'm fawning over him like he never left. Only now I'm even more infatuated with him than I was five years ago. I'm driving myself crazy thinking that maybe he only slept with me because he was desperate. And now he regrets it because he sees that deep down I really am still that same pathetic little girl who used to follow him around like a lost puppy."

"Slow down there, killer." Lily laughs. "One, a man like that doesn't sleep with a girl out of desperation. Seriously, have you looked at him?"

"Um, yeah, pretty sure I have," I deadpan.

"Well then you know what I'm talking about. He could probably sleep with quite literally anyone he wanted to. He slept with you because he wanted to. I don't think he'd risk his friendship with Finn for a piece of ass. And two, you're not a pathetic little girl. You're a grown ass woman who went after what she wanted. There's no shame in that."

"Then why do I feel like I seriously ruined everything?"

"Because you're in it. You're fully invested. And the thought of things not going your way terrifies you."

"You know me too well," I tell her, a trace of a smile pulling at my lips.

"You're just now realizing this?" She laughs. "Listen, if you're that worried about it, talk to him."

"You're right. I need to bite the bullet and do it. Maybe after Finn goes to bed."

"Or, you could do it now," she suggests.

"I can't risk it with Finn home."

"Maybe I can help in that regard." She grins at me from across the table as she grabs her purse and drops it into her lap. Moments later she pulls out her cell phone, sliding her finger across the screen.

"What are you doing?"

"Calling Finn," she tells me, pressing the phone to her ear. "Finn, hey. It's Lily." She smiles, nibbling on her lower lip. "What are you doing right now?" She looks up at me and winks. "You just read my mind. I'll meet you there in twenty." With that, she hangs up the phone, setting the device on the table. "There," she announces. "Problem solved."

"That seemed way too easy."

"It was." She laughs. "Apparently he was getting ready to call me to see if I wanted to have drinks. I'm meeting him at Moe's in twenty minutes."

"Must be nice being old enough to drink." I grimace. I'm a little salty over the fact that she turned twenty-one a few weeks ago and I still have three months to go. Not that I really have any desire to go out drinking. I just like the idea of knowing I can if I want to.

"It really is." She picks up her phone and drops it back into her purse. "Now, let's get the bill paid so you can get home and I can go provide you with some cover."

"Okay. But first I need to get a box."

Fifteen minutes later, I pull into the driveway. Finn's car is still here but I expected as much considering he typically walks to Moe's. Climbing out of the car, I grab my leftovers and purse before knocking the door closed with my hip.

Making my way up to the front porch, I jump, nearly dropping the carryout container when I hear a voice behind me right as I reach the door.

"What did you bring me?"

I swing around to find Ryland coming up the steps behind me.

"Why do you keep doing that?" I bite at him.

"Doing what?" He grins, sliding past me before opening the front door, waiting for me to enter before following me inside.

"Sneaking up on me like that," I tell him, dropping my purse just inside the door.

"I'm not doing it intentionally." He chuckles.

"And it's taco salad," I say, holding up the Styrofoam container. "You want some?"

"I already ate, but thank you." He takes the container from my hand. "I'll stick this in the fridge for you."

"You don't have to do that." But he's already halfway to the kitchen by the time I finish my sentence. Following after him, I enter the room just as he's closing the refrigerator. "What were you doing outside anyway?" I question, leaning against the doorframe.

"I was just checking things out." He turns, pulling out a chair at the kitchen table before taking a seat.

"Checking things out?" I arch a brow at him, pushing away from the door before heading in his direction. I pull out the chair directly across from him and take a seat. "As in you were trying to see if whoever broke in last night was stupid enough to be lurking around."

"Pretty much."

"Well, you and Finn fixed the window and there's no way I'm leaving any doors unlocked anytime soon so I think we'll be good."

"No, I know the house is secure. But the fact still remains that someone did break in."

"Trust me," I lean back in the chair, "I don't need a reminder. I'm well aware that someone was here. I have a half empty underwear drawer to prove it." I cross my arms in front of myself.

An awkward silence settles over us and for the first time in my life I feel like I have no idea what to say. The person who always has something to say about everything is at a loss for words.

"So, did you arrange for Lily to get Finn out of the house so we could sit here and stare at each other or did you have something you wanted to talk about?"

"I didn't…" I start, but then realize that lying is pointless. He clearly already knows the truth. "Fine," I grind out. "You caught me. She called him for me."

"Well, if it makes you feel any better I had convinced him to call her just moments before she called him." He grins.

"You did?" My stomach dances to life. "Why?"

"Because I knew that we needed to talk and that there was no way we were going to be able to do so with Finn here."

"Seems we had the same idea in mind."

"Seems we did." He nods. "So, are you going to talk?"

"Me? You said you needed to talk to me. You start."

"No, I said *we* needed to talk."

"Now you're just splitting hairs. Clearly you had something you wanted to say, so say it."

"You first."

"Ryland." I give him a pointed look.

"Fine. I'll go first." The playfulness fades from his expression. "Last night shouldn't have happened."

"I knew you were going to do this," I interrupt, anger and disappointment building in my chest.

"Before you get all quick tempered on me, maybe you should let me finish." His eyes twinkle with amusement.

"Fine." I gesture for him to continue.

"What I was going to say is, last night shouldn't have happened, *but* I also can't bring myself to regret that it did." He meets my gaze and holds it. "I have no idea what the hell we're doing here, Ainsley. But I do know that whatever it is, I don't want it to stop."

"Neither do I," I admit, relief flooding through me.

"With any other woman I would probably let this ride and see where it goes but I can't do that with you. I have to know going in what it is that you're wanting out of this."

"What I'm wanting out of this?" I crinkle my forehead in confusion. "I thought I was pretty clear with what I want… You."

"That's a pretty broad statement. Is this just sexual? Are you trying to fulfill some childhood fantasy?"

"Are you seriously asking me this right now?"

"Yes, I am. Because if I'm going to risk everything on this, Ainsley, I need to know we're on the same page."

"And what page is that?" I ask, needing him to be the one to set the terms.

"I don't want to just fuck you. Well, I do." He chuckles, lightening the mood slightly. "But that's not all I want. You are not someone's booty call. You are a woman that deserves so much more than that."

"And you want to be the one to give it to me?" I ask, my heart lodged somewhere in my throat.

"I want to be the one that tries."

"What does that even mean?"

"It means that I don't know if I can be the type of man you deserve. I don't know if I'll ever be someone worthy of your love. But I do know that I want to be."

"Ryland, you have been protecting me for most of my life. Why would you ever think you weren't worthy of me? Perhaps it's me who isn't worthy of you."

"You have no idea how precious you are to me, Ains. You never have. I don't expect you to understand how fucking terrified I am that I'm going to hurt you. Even if it's the last thing I want to do. I'm still a guy. And guys do stupid shit sometimes, even if their intentions are good."

"Everyone does stupid shit sometimes. Who's to say I won't be the one to screw it all up?"

"Out of the two of us, my money is on me."

"Well, I'm willing to take the risk." I stand, crossing around the table. "I've wanted you for over half my life. I'd rather this end with you breaking my heart into a million pieces than it end because we were too afraid to try."

"You say that now." He looks up at me, uncertainty clouding his eyes.

"You asked me what I want." I slide down, straddling his lap. "I want you. All of you. The good. The bad. All of it."

"I'm worried that you have some skewed version of me in your head. I'm not the man you think I am."

"Maybe I don't know everything there is to know, but I still know you at your core. I know that you would do anything for me. Five years apart hasn't changed the lifetime we spent before it. You are still Ryland. The boy who would do anything I asked of him. And I am still Ainsley, the girl you've spent your whole life protecting. Sure, things have changed." I smile. "*Obviously*. But I feel like in so many ways we still are those same two people."

"The way you talk, it's like you believe anything is possible."

"When I'm with you it feels like it is."

"So we're really doing this?" I can't tell if he seems more nervous or excited about this fact.

"We're really doing this," I confirm, nodding my head.

"You know." He wraps his arms around my back and tugs me closer. "We can't keep this from Finn forever."

"I know. But that doesn't mean we don't have time to figure things out. We do. And I know that this seems sudden. It does for me, too. And while yes, this all started because I got drunk and couldn't keep my mouth shut, it doesn't change that every word I said was true. This is all I've ever wanted. *You* are all I've ever wanted." I tangle my fingers in his hair. "Now kiss me or I may never shut up."

With that, his mouth closes over mine.

Chapter 17

Ainsley

Five years ago…

I sit in the back of the courtroom, my stomach clenched in knots so tight I feel like I can barely breathe.

Finn doesn't know I'm here. He's seated at the front of the room directly behind Ryland and his attorney.

He didn't want me here. Honestly, I didn't really want to be here, either. But as the morning wore on, I knew I had to be. I had to see him one last time before he's ripped out of my life for good.

So, I skipped school after third period and took the bus, which I also know Finn wouldn't approve of, and I travelled to downtown Detroit by myself.

I don't know why or what I hoped to accomplish by coming here today. After the initial shock of Ryland's arrest had worn off, I became angry. So angry that Finn and I had our first real fight maybe ever. I blamed him. I blamed him for Ryland being arrested. I blamed him for everything, even though I know he had nothing to do with it. And then my anger turned from Finn to Ryland.

I've stewed for weeks, knowing that his sentencing hearing was fast approaching. I thought about all the ways he had done me wrong. Even if what happened had absolutely nothing to do with me, it still feels like I'm the only person being punished.

It's unreasonable and childish, I know, but it's how I feel. My entire life everyone I thought I could count on has left me. My mom, who chose drugs over her own husband and children. My dad, who died, leaving me basically an orphan at age twelve. And now Ryland, my best friend. The boy I have loved for what feels like forever, is leaving me, too. Even though he promised me he never would.

He's a liar. A manipulator. He shows you what he wants you to see. He makes you believe he's this amazing person when in reality he's just as selfish as the rest.

And now it's just us. Just me and Finn. And while I know I should be grateful that I still have my brother, and that Ryland didn't take him down with him, I can't see past my own broken heart to feel anything but anger that's slowly starting to eat away at me.

The judge asks Ryland to stand. I swear it feels like my insides are being twisted around each other. I don't think I've ever been more nervous in my entire life.

I keep waiting, hoping for a miracle I've been told won't come. In the beginning, I refused to accept that there would be any other outcome than Ryland being released with time served. Finn has advised me that is not going to happen. I guess the amount of drugs he intended to sell was quite extensive. Ten years in prison is his possible sentence and no matter how much I try, I can't wrap my head around this fact.

I listen to the judge talk, but I'm not sure I absorb a single word of it. My heart is beating too loudly in my chest. My mouth is dry and my palms feel clammy as I press them together in front of me.

"Seven years." It's the only piece I'm able to grasp through my haze.

Seven years…

Chair legs scrape the floor as officers make their way around the defendant's table to cart Ryland away. He's wearing an orange jumpsuit, his hands handcuffed in front of him.

When they turn to lead him out of the courtroom, I get my first real look at him in months. He hasn't shaved in a couple of weeks and his normally stylish messy hair hangs limp across his forehead.

The sight devastates me and yet serves to further fuel my anger. I want to stand up. I want to scream. I want to tell him how much I hate him for what he did. To Finn. To me. I want to tell him what a liar he is for leaving me. But I can't move. Hell, I can't even breathe. I'm paralyzed. Paralyzed by fear. Paralyzed by disbelief. And paralyzed by the fact that Ryland Thorpe is no longer a part of my life.

I watch him leave the courtroom. I watch him walk away without a backward glance. Leaving me behind just like everyone else has done.

Chapter 18

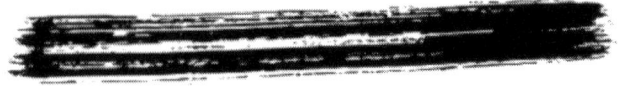

Ainsley

Two weeks. That's how long it's been since my drunken confession to Ryland. Two weeks of heated glances from across the room. Two weeks of *accidental* brushes in the hallway. Two weeks of stolen kisses. Two weeks of secret moments locked away in the confines of my room while Finn sleeps down the hall.

It's been hands down the best two weeks of my life. Truthfully only one thing could make it better. Not having to lie to the only family I have.

I want to tell Finn. Hell, I wanted to tell Finn when it all first began. But I knew if I wanted any chance to figure this out, I had to do it on my own, without his judgement or his concern. I needed time to figure out how I truly felt before I let his opinions sway me one way or the other.

I'm not sure what I thought I needed to figure out, because I feel exactly like I knew I would – floating around on a cloud of happy.

"Knock. Knock." I hear a light tap on my door seconds before it swings open and Ryland appears in the doorway.

I heard him come in from work a little bit ago but since Finn was already home, I decided it was best that I stay in my room and try to finish at least a couple more chapters of the book I was assigned to read for English class.

This is my first week of summer courses, and while it's still school, my course load is a lot lighter this semester. I did that on purpose with the hope of picking up more hours at the diner. Summers are the busiest time of year and as such, I have the ability to earn a lot more in tips. Every summer I try to squeeze all my classes into two to three days if I can, so that I can work longer shifts on the other days.

"Hey." I smile, taking in Ryland's damp hair and his standard, go-to, white tee.

"Hey. What are you doing?"

"Reading." I hold up my book to show him the cover.

"Pride and Prejudice. Haven't you read that book at least a hundred times by now?"

"Try like twice, but it's been a while and since it's for my English class, I thought I should suck it up and re-read it."

"So you're giving yourself a refresher." He grins.

"Pretty much," I agree, dropping the book onto the bed next to me. "What are you doing? Got any exciting plans for this fine Friday evening?"

"Actually, I was thinking about asking this girl if she wanted to grab dinner and go see a movie but now I'm not so sure."

"Why are you not so sure?" I bite down on my bottom lip to keep my smile at bay.

"Well, I know she's extremely busy and I don't want her to feel like she has to say yes."

"I don't think she'd feel that way at all. In fact, I bet she would love an excuse to take a night off. I think you should ask her."

"Yeah?" He cocks his head to the side as he leans against the door frame.

"Definitely."

"Oh for fuck's sake," Finn grumbles as he passes Ryland in the hallway. "Five years has not changed how damn annoying you two are. Just go to a fucking movie already."

Ryland chuckles, his gaze following Finn until he disappears in the living room before swinging back to me.

That's one good thing about my brother, he's completely oblivious. He thinks that Ryland and my behavior is us getting back to the way things used to be. He has no idea that there's this completely new element to our relationship.

"He's being temperamental because Lily blew him off tonight."

"Lily had to work. That's hardly her blowing him off."

"Try telling grouchy ass that." He hitches his thumb down the hall. "Now, where were we before we were rudely interrupted?"

"I believe you were just about to invite me somewhere."

"Ah, yes, that's right." His smile stretches across his face, the beauty of it impossible to ignore. "Ainsley Kenter, would you like to go have dinner and see a movie with me?"

"Well, that depends." I lean forward, pulling my knees to my chest. "Are you going to take me somewhere good?"

"I was thinking Apollo's, but I'm open to suggestions if you're not feeling burgers."

"Actually, Apollo's sounds amazing. But the movie… This is make or break it for me."

"*Silent Ascent*, obviously. You can't go wrong when you mix sexy sororities with a human possessing demon."

"Now I know you're messing with me." I give him a pointed look.

"Okay, you got me. I was actually thinking maybe we could catch the new Tarantino movie. I know how much you like his stuff."

"Sold," I announce loudly, quickly sliding off the edge of the bed. "Give me fifteen minutes and I'll be ready," I say, shooing him out of my doorway before pushing the door closed.

"Have the burgers here always been this good or is it because it's been so long since I've had one?" Ryland asks, sinking his teeth into his already half eaten burger, even though mine is still sitting untouched on my plate. I'm a fries first kind of girl.

"I think maybe both." I giggle.

"I'm serious. This burger is amazing," he says, swallowing and then instantly going in for another bite.

So much about this is familiar. Sitting across the booth from Ryland. The jukebox playing softly in the background. The tacky and yet oddly appealing décor of Apollo's. This used to be our place, once upon a time. In fact, whenever we'd do anything together, ninety-five percent of the time we'd end up here afterward.

"Well I for one think the fries blow the burgers out of the water. I forgot how good hand cut fries are versus frozen ones."

"Forgot? How long has it been since you've been here? You used to love coming to this place."

"Five years."

"What?" He gives me a weird look as he pops the last bite of his burger into his mouth.

"You asked how long it's been since I've been here. It's been about five and a half years. Since the last time you brought me here to be exact."

"Wait. You mean to tell me you haven't been here since the day I took you ice skating on the lake and you fell and we thought you had broken your hand?"

My chest swells. I hadn't considered for even a second that he would remember the last time we were here together. After so many visits, you would think they would all blend together. Then again, I did spend half the day thinking I had broken my hand so it wasn't our typical visit.

"I refused to let you take me to the ER because I didn't want to land Finn with a huge hospital bill if I didn't have to."

"So Patti brought you out a bucket of ice and made you sit with your hand in it the whole time we were eating so we could see if we could get the swelling down."

We both smile at the memory.

"How is it possible that it's been that long ago since that day?" he thinks aloud. "Sometimes I forget how much time has passed."

"Yeah, me too," I admit, finding this even truer as of late.

There are times that I'll be sitting on the couch and I'll look over at him and still feel like that same teenage girl. The one whose heart would pick up speed every time our eyes would lock and how I would lose myself in daydreams about him grabbing me and kissing me.

"Why did you stop coming here?" He pulls me from my thoughts and I look up to see his face has sobered.

"I guess it didn't feel right without you." I shrug, popping a fry into my mouth and chewing slowly.

He thinks over my words for a long moment.

"I'm really sorry, Ainsley."

"Don't." I stop him before he can say more. "I don't want to think about days past or years wasted. I just want to enjoy this. Being back here with you again. Speaking of which." I pick up my knife and cut my burger down the middle, plopping half of it onto his plate moments later.

"Still can't eat the whole burger, huh?" He chuckles, glancing down at his plate before his eyes come back up to mine.

"Nope. And if I recall, you can easily eat all of yours and half of mine. I'm assuming that hasn't changed."

"I don't know. I didn't eat nearly as much in prison. I think my stomach may have shrunk a little."

"So are you telling me you're not going to eat half of my burger like you always used to?"

"No, I'm definitely going to eat it. I'm just saying it might be a little more difficult than it used to be." He picks up the sandwich and takes a massive bite.

"You're exactly as I remember." My thoughts coming out without me intending them to.

"What do you mean?" he asks around a mouthful of food.

"I don't know. You were gone for so long. Sometimes I thought maybe I had imagined how cute and funny you were. In fact, I had convinced myself that when, or if, I ever saw you again I'd realize immediately that the feelings I thought I harbored for you was some stupid teenage crush and that you'd turn out to be a complete douche."

"Is that your way of saying you don't think I'm a douche?" His shoulders shake with laughter but no sound comes out of his mouth.

"I guess so." I shrug, picking up another fry.

"Well, I guess that's good to know." He watches me slide the fry through ketchup before dropping it into my mouth. "And the stupid teenage crush?"

"Not stupid. And not a crush. Something much, much more than that."

"I still can't believe I had no idea that you felt that way about me."

"I buried it pretty deep. Truthfully, I would have been mortified if you had found out back then."

"And now."

"I think you know where I stand now." I give him a knowing look.

"So we're two weeks in… No regrets yet?"

"Not a single one," I answer with complete honesty. "You?"

"Not for even a second."

"Careful, Mr. Thorpe. You might have me thinking you're starting to fall for me," I say playfully.

"There's no starting to. I've done swan dived off a hundred-foot cliff."

I swear, if it was socially acceptable to stand up on a booth and scream out in joy while I danced around like a lunatic, I would not be sitting still in my seat right now, trying to act like what he just said hasn't skyrocketed my feelings to a whole other level.

"I want to tell Finn," he adds before I have too much time to celebrate the victory he just handed to me.

"Not yet." I shake my head.

I don't know why the thought of telling my brother terrifies the hell out of me. It's not like he isn't currently dating *my* best friend. He would have absolutely no room to talk. But unfortunately his opinion means a lot more to me than I wish it did. And I know it does for Ryland, too.

I think deep down we both know that without Finn's blessing, we don't stand a chance. And I'm just not ready to rip that Band-Aid off yet.

"Ainsley." He leans back in the booth, lifting his beer bottle to his lips.

"Don't look at me like that, Ryland. It's been two weeks. We're still figuring things out. I don't want to drag Finn into this yet."

"Do you like me?" he asks, setting his beer on the table.

"What kind of question is that? You know I do."

"Do you want to be with me?"

"Again, you already know I do."

"Then I don't understand the hold up."

"I just want to enjoy this a little longer. I know it probably sounds bad, but I like knowing something that no one else knows. I want to live in this secret bubble for a little longer."

I can tell he's not entirely convinced with my reasoning but for whatever reason, he chooses not to push the issue further.

"Fine. But I want to tell him soon. The longer this goes on the more of a chance he's going to murder me when the truth finally comes out."

"Oh please." I swipe my hand through the air. "You can totally take him."

"He's my best friend, Ains. I don't feel right keeping this from him."

"I know. Soon," I promise. "Now can we please stop talking about my brother?"

"Fine." He smiles, finishing off the remainder of his beer. "I'm going to need an extra stomach to get through the rest of this food." He gestures down to his plate where part of my burger and all of his fries still sit."

"I have confidence in you."

"I make no promises that I won't conk out during the movie. I might go into a food coma."

"I'm pretty sure I can think of a few ways to keep you awake." I raise my eyebrows up and down at him.

"Keep talking like that and we might not even make it to the movie."

"In that case." I run my finger across my mouth like I'm zipping my lips together.

"I see how it is. You're choosing Tarantino over me."

"Maybe. Or maybe I just really want to make out with you in a dark theater." I nibble on my bottom lip. "Bucket list and all."

"Making out in a theater is on your bucket list?" He scrunches his face.

"No. Making out with *you* in a theater is on my bucket list. Then again, in all fairness, making out with you anywhere is likely to check a box or two."

"What else is on this bucket list of yours?" He drops his elbows onto the table and leans forward.

"Guess you'll have to stick around and find out," I tell him, popping another fry into my mouth.

"Guess I will." He smiles, challenge in his eyes.

"Did you really not like it?" I ask, knocking my shoulder into Ryland's as we exit the theater.

"I liked every single second of it. Just none of the movie." He gives me a seductive look.

I may or may not have spent most of the movie feeling him up through his jeans. Truthfully, I wanted to do a lot more but since I kept catching the older couple next to us looking at me, I had to keep it low key.

"Did you even watch it?"

"Of course I did. Now did I retain any of it is the real question."

"Ryland." I shove him playfully.

"What?" He chuckles. "I was a little distracted."

"That's the last time I go to a movie with you," I joke, knowing I'd go sit through another two hour movie with him right now.

Ryland opens his mouth like he's about to say something, but then instantly snaps it closed as he comes to an abrupt halt. Turning my attention forward, my jaw nearly hits the concrete when my gaze locks with Oscar, standing directly in front of us.

"Oscar," I choke out past the sudden knot lodged in my throat. "What are you doing here?" I ask, not able to think of a single other thing to say.

"Seeing a movie." He gestures to the theater behind me.

"Right. Of course." I shake my head. "I'm just surprised to see you. I didn't realize you were back from Ohio. I thought you stayed there for the summer break."

"Normally I do, but I decided to come home this year." He tries to act casual but there's something tense in his features.

"Gotcha. Well, if you're seeing the Tarantino movie, it's good. I recommend it."

"Is that what you guys saw?" His eyes dart to Ryland, reminding me that he's standing next to me.

"Yeah, it is." I rock back on my heels. "Sorry, I forgot you two have never met. Ryland, this is Oscar. Oscar, this is Finn's best friend, Ryland."

"The one that was in prison." Oscar nods, giving Ryland a quick once over as if he's trying to size him up.

"That's me," Ryland answers smoothly. "Sorry, but I have no idea who you are. Guess that tells me everything I need to know."

My gaze swings to Ryland and I'm not sure if I want to high five him or punch the smug look off his face. I've never seen him be so outwardly rude before. Not that Oscar doesn't deserve that and so much more, but Ryland doesn't know that.

"He's just messing with you." I laugh nervously. "Well, we should probably get going. Finn will be expecting us back soon." I snake my arm through Ryland's and pull him alongside me. "It was good seeing you again, Oscar," I lie, not looking back as I practically drag Ryland through the parking lot.

"Finn's best friend? That's how you introduce me." He stops just shy of my car and whips around to face me.

"I'm sorry about that. I was trying to downplay it in front of Oscar."

"What the fuck for?"

"It's…" I shuffle my feet. "It's complicated. Oscar and I dated for a while and he's an extremely jealous person so I was trying to ruffle as few of his feathers as possible."

"What do you mean he's extremely jealous?" Ryland's aggravation quickly morphs into concern.

"Just that. He's jealous."

"When you say you dated him…" He gives me a look I pick up on instantly.

"Oh my god, Ryland. Yes, he is the guy I lost my virginity to. The only other guy I've slept with to be exact. Anything else you'd like to know?"

"You gave *him* your virginity?" He points back toward the theater. "Fuck, I don't even know the guy but one look at him and I knew immediately that he's a douche bag of epic proportion."

"Well, I guess I'm not wired with the same Spidey sense as you." I uncross my arms and then cross them again, growing increasingly more uncomfortable with this conversation.

"So what happened then?" he asks.

It takes a moment for my brain to process what he's asking. "You mean between me and Oscar?"

"Yeah." He nods.

"Nothing. We dated a few months. Broke up. He left for college. End of story."

"So you haven't seen him since he left?"

"I saw him a few weeks ago when he was in town for a baseball tournament."

"So he's a jock. Makes more sense now."

"What does?"

"Nothing." He shakes his head.

"Listen, this whole territorial thing you've got going on is cute and all, but Oscar is not a threat. Hell, he's not even a blip on the radar. I'm not being dramatic when I say that the day he left for college was one of the happiest days of my life."

Ryland steps toward me. "I take it things didn't end well?" He slides his hand under my chin and forces my face up.

"That's one way to put it."

"Did he hurt you?"

"What? No." I have no choice but to lie. With no idea of what Ryland would do if he found out the truth about what kind of guy Oscar really is. Douche bag doesn't even begin to cover it.

"You'd tell me if he did, right?" His eyes bore into mine.

"Yes, of course." I have to force the words out, praying to God they sound even remotely believable. "Now, can we please get out of here? We started something in the theater that I would very much like to finish."

"Oh would you now?" His expression relaxes as his sexy smile slides back into place. "Tell me," he leans down, brushing his lips against mine, "where is sex in a car on that bucket list of yours?"

"Right now, it's at the very top." I smile, forgetting all about Oscar the second Ryland's tongue slides into my mouth.

Chapter 19

Ainsley

"Hey, Ains. Have you seen my gray button down? The one with the collar," Finn asks, poking his head into the laundry room where I'm currently switching over my clothes from the washer to the dryer.

"You mean the only button down you own?" I tease, turning to retrieve it off the back of the door where I hung it earlier today. "You left it in the dryer," I tell him, shoving it in his direction. "Got a hot date or something?"

"A job interview actually."

"A job interview?" I question, surprised. "I didn't know you were looking for a new job."

"I wasn't. Well, not really. But Lily introduced me to this guy she knows who works at Smithville Auto Mall selling cars at the Lexus dealership. Apparently, they're looking for a couple new sales guys."

"A car salesman?" I give him a funny look, having a hard time picturing my brother selling cars.

"Why not? You'd be hard pressed to find someone who knows more about cars than I do. Besides, the money's good."

"*If* you sell cars the money is good."

"Which I will. Plus, with this job I'll be able to quit my other jobs and just work one job like a normal person."

"Since when have you cared about being normal?"

"Is it so wrong that I want to work a normal five day a week job and not spend every waking minute earning nickels and dimes at dead end jobs that will never get me anywhere?"

"Of course not." I instantly lighten my approach, seeing that I've struck a nerve. "But you're going to need more than one nice shirt if you get the job," I tease.

"I'm aware of this, thanks," he grumbles, spinning around before heading back into the kitchen.

I close the dryer and turn it on before following after him.

"So what time is this interview of yours?" I ask, picking up the basket of clean clothes I left sitting on the kitchen table.

"At four."

"So that's why you're home early."

"Yes and no. Jim needed someone to work this weekend so I told him I'd work a half day

Saturday if he was good with me taking a half day today. That was actually before I knew I had the interview."

"How's he going to feel if you end up leaving? You've been working there since you were a teenager."

"I think he'll be happy for me. I started working there to earn a little extra cash. I never dreamed it would turn into a full-time gig."

"Well, you also never thought you'd be responsible for raising a twelve-year-old when you were only eighteen," I say, reminding myself of just how much my brother has sacrificed for me.

"True." He drapes his shirt over the back of a kitchen chair before heading toward the refrigerator. "I'd do it all again though," he says, his back to me. "But, you're not a kid anymore, Ains, and I think it's about time I start doing things for myself." He pulls out a Pepsi and pops the top of the can as he turns back toward me.

"I couldn't agree more." I smile, wondering what the hell has gotten into my brother. But then I remember a certain someone in his life that is having quite the impact.

When this whole Lily thing started I didn't think it would ever get off the ground, but boy was I wrong. They both seem quite smitten with each other and now here's Finn, trying to move up in the world by getting a new job. One that could potentially change his financial future if he turns out to be successful at it.

"For what it's worth, I'm proud of you," I tell him, wishing I hadn't reacted so negatively when he told me about his interview.

"You are?" He grins, taking a sip of his soda.

"I am. It's about time you start thinking about *your* future. Like you said, I'm not a kid anymore. Soon I'll be a college graduate that will hopefully be able to land a decent job and get a place of my own."

"Or you can stay here with me forever." He shrugs. "Just saying."

"You'd like that too much, Mr. Overprotective." I roll my eyes.

"Speaking of overprotective men, has Ryland seemed a little weird to you recently?"

A nervous pit hollows inside my stomach. "No, why?"

"I don't know. He just seems a little off. Distracted, I guess, is the right word. You've been hanging out with him more than I have. Certainly you've noticed it, too."

"I think he's still adjusting." I try to seem completely at ease, even though on the inside I'm freaking out a little. "He's only been home a few weeks. I think he's still finding his footing."

"Has he said anything to you about seeing someone?"

"Seeing someone?" I choke on the words. "No. I don't think he's seeing anyone. Or at least, not that he's told me. Why?"

"I don't know. I just get the impression there's something else going on. If he hasn't said anything then it must be serious."

"Why would saying something make it less serious?" I question his logic. "You would think if it were *that* serious he'd want to tell his family." I gesture between the two of us.

"Maybe. Or maybe he's afraid if he says something it will jinx it."

"Jinx it?" I give him a doubtful look. "Since when has Ryland Thorpe ever been superstitious? Do you really think he would intentionally not tell us something if it was important to him?"

"I don't know. He's different since he got out of jail."

"Of course he is. He spent five years locked in a prison cell. That's sure to change anyone."

"I know that. Of course I do. It's just, at first he seemed like normal Ryland. The same dude I've known my entire life. But the last couple of weeks he seems distant. It's fucking weird."

"Maybe it took being out for a few days for it to really sink in." I shrug, grasping at straws at this point.

"Maybe." He sighs. "But you two seem to be getting back on track. I knew once he was home you wouldn't be able to stay mad at him. You two were always thick as thieves."

"Yeah. It took me a little while but we're getting there. I forgot how much I loved having him around. I don't think I realized just how much I actually missed him."

"Well, he missed you, too. Every time I went to see him you were the very first person he asked about."

"I was?" I smile, trying not to act too overly excited by this news.

"You were," he confirms, looking at the time on the wall clock behind me. "Shit, is it already three?"

I glance at the clock before turning back toward him. "Yep."

"Shit, I gotta get ready." He grabs his shirt and heads across the kitchen, pausing in the doorway. "You'll let me know if Ryland says anything to you about what's going on with him, yeah?"

"I will," I confirm, feeling extremely guilty for continuing to lie to my brother, especially since he's starting to pick up on Ryland acting different.

"Thanks, Ains."

"Good luck at your interview. I'll keep my fingers crossed for you," I call after him as he heads out of the kitchen.

"Thank you," he hollers back before he disappears around the corner. Seconds later, I hear the bathroom door shut.

Taking in a deep breath, I slowly let it out before grabbing my laundry basket off the table. Propping it onto my hip, I head toward my room, an uneasy feeling settling deep in my gut.

"Everything okay?" Lily slides up next to me where I'm busy cleaning tables as I close down the dining room.

It's rare that I pick up a closing shift, but after my run in with Finn yesterday I was eager to have a reason to avoid going home after class today. I hate lying to him. Almost as much as I hate asking Ryland to lie to him.

"Yeah, everything is fine. Why?" I move to the next table, spraying cleaner across the top.

"You've been really quiet today. Is everything okay with Ryland?"

"Everything is really good with Ryland," I answer honestly. In fact, other than the fact that we're lying to the person closest to us, things couldn't be much better.

We've gone out several times together, revisiting some of our favorite spots from when we were younger. I feel like we've reconnected on a level I never thought we'd get back to again.

"So then why do I get the feeling something is off with you?" Lily knows me too well to take me at my word.

"I think Finn is starting to suspect something," I tell her, stopping mid-wipe to look at her. "He asked me yesterday if I had noticed anything off with Ryland. He thinks maybe he's dating someone and for whatever reason isn't ready to tell any of us."

"Yeah, he mentioned something of that nature to me as well. But he didn't seem worried about it or anything. Maybe it just freaked you out because you know what's actually going on."

"Maybe," I admit. "I just feel so bad. I thought keeping this from him would be easy, but the longer it goes on the sicker I feel about it."

"Well, you and Ryland have only been seeing each other, if that's what we're calling it, for a few weeks. Things are still new. It's not too late to tell him, ya know."

"You say it like it's just that simple. What am I supposed to say, *hey Finn, remember when you asked me if Ryland was acting weird? Well, the reason he's acting that way is because we've been sleeping together and hiding it from you. You're welcome.*" I phrase overly cheery and dramatic.

"Well, maybe don't use those exact words." She chuckles.

"I'm serious, Lily. I know it's a conversation that needs to be had, but I have no idea how to even broach the subject. It's horrible. I've never had any issue talking to Finn about anything before. But this, I don't know. I'm scared."

"Listen, I know it's not going to be an easy conversation, but you need to do everyone involved a favor and have it. Once it's out in the open then that's that."

"And if Finn loses his mind?"

"Then he loses his mind."

"Says the person who doesn't have any stake in the game."

"I don't have any stake in the game?" Her expression instantly shifts. "Have you forgotten that you're not the only one keeping things from Finn? I've known about you and Ryland from the beginning and I haven't said a word. How do you think he's going to take that news? Knowing that not only were his sister and best friend lying to him, but so was his girlfriend?"

"Girlfriend? I didn't realize you guys were officially official," I snip, taking my frustration out on her when she's the last person that deserves it. "And perhaps you should have thought about that before you started dating your best friend's brother. Kind of takes conflict of interest to a whole new level."

"Why don't you tell me how you really feel, Ains?" She takes a full step back, anger tugging at her features.

"Pretty sure I just did," I grumble, resuming wiping down the table.

"Wow." She lets out an angry laugh. "Listen, I get that you're stressed out and you're worried about telling Finn, but taking your shit out on me isn't helping your situation. If your plan is to alienate everyone, you're well on your way to achieving your goal."

With that, she spins around and storms off.

I straighten and call after her, "Lily."

She doesn't turn around as she slams the kitchen door open and disappears moments later.

I know I should go after her, apologize, but for some reason I can't bring myself to do it. Being angry with myself has bled into me being angry with Lily for absolutely no reason at all.

So what if she's dating Finn. I'm actually happy for the two of them. And she's right. She's lying to her boyfriend for me, which isn't fair of me to ask her to do. And yet she's still doing it, despite the fact that it could blow up her entire relationship when Finn finds out.

Maybe I'm overreacting. Maybe Finn will take the news just as I did when I found out about him and Lily. Maybe he'll be a little surprised and caught off guard, but at the end of the day he'll realize that we make each other happy and that will be enough for him.

But even I know that's wishful thinking.

Finn raised me. Finn gave up some of the best years of his life to make sure I didn't end up in the foster care system. Finn worked countless hours at crappy jobs to make enough money to keep us afloat. And I repay him with secrets and lies.

I know how protective Finn is of me. I also know how well he knows Ryland, which means he's witnessed the worst parts of him. But at the same time, that also means he knows the best parts of him. And he obviously trusts him with me. Hell, Ryland helped raise me right alongside Finn.

Honestly, I'm not sure if that hurts or helps my case.

I watch Lily leave a few minutes later. I know I should go after her but I'm too wrapped up in my own head to bother making things right with my best friend. That should be my first indication that I've gone astray.

When I head out of the restaurant nearly thirty minutes later, I've made the decision that Finn deserves the truth and that I need to be the one to tell him. I know Ryland is his best friend, but I'm his sister, *his family*, and I owe it to him to be the one to do it.

I don't know how or when exactly, but I know it needs to be soon. And while the thought makes me extremely nervous, I also feel good about the decision. There's only one thing holding me back from having a real relationship with Ryland and this is it.

As I head across the street toward the dark parking lot where my car is parked, I get an eerie feeling that I'm being watched. I don't know how to explain it other than the way the small hairs on the back of my neck stand up and this weird feeling in the pit of my stomach.

Quickening my strides, I jog the remaining few feet to my car, not able to get the door open fast enough. I quickly duck inside and pull the door closed, clicking the locks in place.

Staring out into the darkness, there's nothing that catches my eye. No movement that I can see.

As I jam the keys into the ignition and start my car, I let out a slow breath, chalking it up to my mind playing tricks on me. A moment later my car sputters to life.

Clicking on the headlights, I let out an audible scream when I catch sight of someone standing in front of my car. It takes me several seconds to realize that it's my co-worker, Davis. He holds his hands up as if to say *I come in peace* before gesturing to the material in his hand.

Realizing what it is, I roll down my window as Davis makes his way around my car.

"Sorry if I scared you." He extends my cardigan to me. Even though it's summer, the restaurant is always freezing, so I typically bring a sweater with me to work to put on if I get cold. "You left this in the back."

"Thank you." I take the article of clothing from him.

"You headed home?"

"Yeah, I've got class early in the morning," I tell him, throwing the sweater into the passenger seat.

"Gotcha." He shoves his hands into the front pockets of his pants. "Anyway I could interest you in dinner this weekend?" he asks.

"That's sweet of you to ask, Davis, but I don't think I can." I let him down easy, the same way I have every time he's asked me out, which has been a lot over the few months we've worked together.

"Too much schoolwork?" he guesses.

"Well that, and I'm kind of seeing someone," I admit. I know it's a baby step, but it feels good to say it out loud so I don't stop there. "It's getting kind of serious and I don't think he would take too lightly to me having dinner with another guy."

"Say no more." He gives me an easy smile. "But if things don't work out, you know where to find me." He nods, taking a step back. "And for what it's worth, he's a lucky guy."

"Goodnight, Davis." I laugh lightly, rolling up the window.

He throws me a small wave before spinning around and heading across the lot to where his car is. I wait until he's climbed into the driver's seat before popping my car into drive and quickly pulling out of the lot.

Chapter 20

Ryland

"You're in a good mood," I observe, watching Finn practically skip out of Jim's office.

"Just put in my notice." He smiles, stopping next to the car I'm working on.

"You got the job?"

"I got the job." He nods.

"Man, that's awesome." I resist the urge to bump his fist, considering my hands are pretty fucking grease covered at the moment. "Congrats."

"Thank you."

"We should celebrate."

"We should. But it will have to wait. I promised Jim I'd pick up a half day tomorrow in exchange for him letting me take a half day yesterday."

"You just put in your notice and you're still picking up weekend shifts." I shake my head at him. "Overachiever."

"I prefer to think of it as I'm a man of my word."

"Well I'm proud of you. It's about time you branched out and did something for yourself."

"Thanks. I thought so, too."

"Anything spurring on this sudden change of heart? I have to say, I thought you were a lifer here."

"I just want more, ya know." He shrugs.

"Lily wouldn't have anything to do with this, would she?" I give him a knowing smirk.

"Maybe a little," he admits, rocking back on his heels. "But more than anything I think I need a change. I'm sick of working my hands to the bone for pennies. It's about time I cashed into something a little more profitable." His eyes dart to my hands.

"Trust me, I totally get it. I'll probably be working here for the rest of my life."

His expression instantly falls.

"Shit, dude. I'm sorry. Here I am rubbing my success in your face when it's my fault you're in this predicament to begin with."

"It's not your fault," I immediately cut him off. "I made a choice and I stand by that choice."

"I'll never be able to repay you for what you did for me, you know that, right? Seriously, I don't know what I would have done…"

"Don't," I cut him off. "We've been over this countless times. What's done is done. Besides, you should be focused on you right now. Hot girlfriend. Fancy new job. Things are really starting to look up for Finn Kenter." I pick up the rag off my cart and wipe my hands.

Finn chuckles. "What about you? I feel like you've been kind of MIA recently. You wouldn't happen to be seeing some hot girl of your own now, would ya?"

Guilt punches me square in the gut. "Nah, you know me. I'm not much for settling down." I shrug, knowing that up until recently the statement would have been true.

I've never been a one-woman man. In fact, until now I can't say that I've ever been in a completely monogamous relationship. Then again, I've never met a woman that made me want to be. That is, until Ainsley.

She's different. She's always been different than all the other girls. She makes me want to be different, too. Better, if that's possible.

"I thought that about myself at one time but look at me now." Finn lightly hits my shoulder. "Just takes meeting the right woman."

I desperately want to tell him that I *have* met her. That she's someone I never expected but was standing in front of me all this time. Hell, I almost do. I almost utter the words. But then I think about the fallout of that confession and decide that now is not the time or place. Besides, Ainsley was very adamant when we spoke last night that she wanted to be the one to tell him.

As much as I feel like it should be me, a conversation between two best friends, she didn't agree. And I care enough about her to back her on this. She's right. This is her family. A family I haven't been a part of for the better part of five years.

But I'm ready for it to all be out in the open. As much as I've enjoyed our weeks of sneaking around, I'm ready to take our relationship public. I want the entire world to know that she is mine, including Finn. No matter what that means for us.

Even if he's pissed, I know eventually he'll forgive me. He has to. Because giving up Ainsley isn't something I'm willing to consider.

"Well, I guess I should get back to the grind. If I want Jim to pay me for my last two weeks I might actually have to get some work done."

"Sounds good, man." I nod, watching him walk away moments later.

The rest of the day goes by at a snail's pace. I'm in a shit mood when I finally leave the shop nearly thirty minutes after closing time. Everyone but Jim has left for the day, which isn't unusual. He's always the first one here and the last to leave.

"Hey." I look up as I cross the lot, surprised when I see Ainsley's old Malibu sitting in the parking lot, her ass leaning against the hood looking so damn sexy it takes everything in me not to pull her into my arms when I reach her.

"Hey. What are you doing here?" I stop directly in front of her. The sight of her significantly improving my mood.

"I picked up the lunch shift after class. Finished up a little while ago and thought I'd swing by and see if you needed a ride home."

"I was just going to walk," I tell her, which is what I do most days. The shop is only about a fifteen-minute walk from the house and I like the time alone to think.

"Well not anymore." She hits me with a stunning smile as she pushes away from the car. "Come on. Get in." She crosses around to the passenger side. "You're driving," she explains when I hit her with a questioning look.

"You sure you want to trust me with your baby? I'm a little rusty."

"My baby. Please, if you wreck this piece of crap you'd be doing me a favor." She laughs. "Now get in."

"Okay." I chuckle, crossing around to the driver's side before opening the door. It makes a horrible creaking sound. "What the hell is wrong with your door?" I ask, cringing at the noise.

"It's done that forever." She leans across the console to look up at me.

"Well that simply won't do." I slide down into the seat and fire the engine to life. Dropping the car into gear, I pull the car forward, pulling into the open garage door rather than onto the street.

"What the hell are you doing?" she asks when I kill the engine.

"I'm going to fix this fucking door," I tell her, climbing out of the car moments later.

Jim comes out of the office as Ainsley gets out of the passenger side. His gaze swings from me to her and then back to me.

"What are you two doing?" he asks curiously.

"Ainsley has something going on with her door. Mind if I hang out for a few and take a look? I can lock up when we're done."

"Fine by me." He nods, crossing around the car to Ainsley. "My lord, girl, you get prettier and prettier every day." He pulls her into a hug.

"Hi, Jim." She grins.

"I trust you more than I trust him," he tells her, jerking his thumb in my direction. "Make sure he doesn't forget to shut the lights off."

"You can count on me," she promises, smiling.

"Really, Jim?" I call after him as he walks away. I watch his shoulders shake with laughter but he doesn't turn back around. Seconds later he exits out of the open garage door, leaving Ainsley and me alone in the shop.

"There," I announce less than ten minutes later, opening the driver's side door. It opens smooth and easy without a sound to be heard. "All fixed."

"If I had known it would be that easy, I would have had Finn fix it ages ago." She closes the door and then opens it again, her smile widening when it once again makes no noise.

"Are you saying that anyone could have done this job? And here I was feeling special," I tease, wrapping an arm around her waist before pulling her to me.

"What? Of course you're the only one that could have done it." She laughs. "My hero."

"Now you're just being a little smart ass." I grab a handful of her ass cheek and squeeze.

She lets out a little yelp, her hands sliding around the back of my neck.

"Perhaps I owe you a proper thank you." She leans in, running her nose along mine.

"I think you do." I grin, pressing a soft kiss to her mouth. "Of course, I can think of a few ways you can thank me without uttering a single word." I turn, pressing her against the side of the car.

"I think I like the way you think." She giggles against my lips.

"What the fuck?" My entire body tenses at the sound.

Ainsley and I break apart so fast that I knock into my tool cart and send it flying into the stone pillar a couple feet away. The tools clang around and send a vibration of noise spiraling through the otherwise silent garage.

When my gaze swings upward, I see Finn stalking toward me, his gaze murderous. I have zero time to react before his hands tangle in my shirt and he halls me backward against the car, barely missing Ainsley as she jumps out of the way. My back slams into the door, the side view mirror catching my side.

"What the fuck?" he screams in my face, pulling me forward a few inches to slam me into the car a second time.

"Finn!" Ainsley yells seconds before I see her tiny hands wrap around his bicep in an effort to pull him off of me. "Let go of him."

"My fucking sister." He shakes Ainsley off, all his rage pinned directly at me.

"I can explain." I try to keep my voice level and even.

"Explain," he snarls, rearing back seconds before his fist connects with the side of my face, snapping my head to the side. "Explain to me why I show up here to see if you want to grab a beer only to find you making out with my little sister."

I've barely recovered from the first blow before he lays the second. I feel the skin below my eye split open, and even though every bone in my body is screaming for me to fight back, I refuse to raise a hand to him.

"Finn, let him go!" Ainsley tries again, this time grabbing his forearm as she pulls with all her might. It doesn't do her a bit of good, but that doesn't stop her from trying.

"I fucking trusted you!" he screams in my face. "I trusted you!"

"Finn. I said stop!" Ainsley screams so loud that he has no choice but to acknowledge her.

His gaze moves to her.

"You have exactly five seconds to get the fuck out of this garage," he warns.

"Or what?" She steps in closer. "What, Finn?" She shoves at him. "Are you going to ground me? Take me home and spank my butt? Or are you going to punch me next? What? What are you going to do?"

He shoves me against the car door again before he releases me, stepping toward his sister.

"I'm not going to tell you again, Ainsley. Go the fuck home."

"Fuck you!" She steps up to him, poking him in the chest with her pointer finger. "You don't get to tell me what to do."

"The fuck I don't. You live under my roof."

"So what? That gives you a right to tell me who I can and cannot be with?"

"Be with?" He chokes over the words. "You're telling me you actually want to be with him?" He cranes his neck in my direction, the disgust on his face unlike anything I've ever seen before.

"Yes, that's exactly what I'm telling you. And had you not come barging in here like some damn wild animal I was going to tell you just that when I got home tonight."

"How long has this been going on?"

"It doesn't matter how long it's been going on," she fires back. "What matters is that I'm in love with him." Her admission doesn't just shock Finn, it shocks the shit out of me as well.

Sure, she's said she was in love with me when she was younger, but I never took it for she was *actually* in love with me. Instead, more of a dramatic way of saying she really liked me. To hear her say it now catches me more by surprise than it probably should.

"You're in love with him?" Finn draws back, hurt and shock registering through his whole body.

"I am. I love him and I want to be with him and you're going to accept that whether you want to or not."

"Like hell I am. This ends now." His face turns to me seconds before his finger is in my face. "Do you fucking hear me?"

"You don't get to do that, Finn." Ainsley steps between us. "You don't get to bully your way into what you want. Ryland and I want to be together and there isn't a thing you can do about it?"

"No?" he snarls.

"No." She stands her ground.

If I wasn't so fucking stunned by the sudden turn this evening has taken, I might actually be impressed by her strong will. Another reminder that this is most certainly not the same soft-spoken little girl she once was.

"Is that what you want?" His gaze flies to me. "You want to be with my fucking sister?"

"Finn."

"Don't fucking Finn me, Ryland. Answer the fucking question."

"Yes."

He takes a full step back, his eyes going back and forth between me and Ainsley.

"So that's how it's going to be. Years of friendship and you're going to choose her."

"There isn't a choice. You are my best friend. And she," I stop myself from saying something I can't take back, "I want you both in my life. I *need* you both in my life."

"If that was true you wouldn't have been fucking my baby sister, in my house, behind my back. You practically helped me raise her. What kind of sick fuck does that?"

His words cut deeper than I thought they would. Mainly because a part of me knows he's right.

"Stop it, Finn." Ainsley cuts in again. "I'm not a little girl anymore. Ryland and I are both adults and we have done nothing wrong."

"Except lie to me."

"So we lied. Boo fucking hoo." Ainsley keeps going. "I'm sorry we lied, but Jesus, you're acting like we committed some cardinal sin. What about you and Lily? How is that any different?"

"Lily isn't a part of this family. Lily did not help raise me. Lily and I did not hide anything from you. Lily wasn't living under your roof all the while betraying you at the same time. The two are nothing alike and you fucking know it."

"No, what I know is you do whatever the hell you want with no regard for how it will make other people feel, but when the shoe is on the other foot you lose your fucking mind."

"That's enough, Ainsley." His nostrils flare. "Go the fuck home. Now!" he says through gritted teeth.

"Make me," she challenges.

"Finn, if we could just talk." I try again but he's having none of it.

"Fuck you, Ryland. You are no longer welcome in *my* home and we are no longer brothers."

Considering everything I've done for him, his words slice me to the bone.

"When this all blows up in your face and he fucks you over," his focus shifts to Ainsley, "don't come crying to me because for once in your life, I won't be there to pick up the fucking pieces."

"Well lucky for me I don't need you to. I'm a big girl. I think I can manage." She crosses her arms in front of her chest, and even though she's trying really hard to hold it together, I can hear the quiver in her voice.

"Good, because I'm done. You're on your own now."

"Finn, wait," I start but his murderous gaze stops me before I can say anything else.

"Fuck you," he says, his voice riddled with defeat. "Fuck you both," he repeats, shaking his head as he spins and exits the garage.

Chapter 21

Ainsley

"I…" I turn toward Ryland, the adrenaline that surged through my veins moments ago giving away to the absolute devastation in my heart.

Ryland's face is pale, making the blood dripping from the gash under his eye that much more prominent.

Without a word, Ryland pulls me into his arms. It's only seconds before I disintegrate into a ball of hysterics in his embrace.

I'm not even sure why I'm crying. Because I'm hurt. Because Finn is hurt. Because Ryland is hurt. Or maybe it's because for the first time in my life, my brother looked at me like he had no idea who I was.

I expected him to be a little upset about Ryland and me, but I never expected him to react as violently as he did.

"I'm so sorry." I sob into Ryland's chest, feeling like I'm to blame for all of this. Had I just listened to him and went to Finn when all this started maybe we could have avoided this.

"You have nothing to apologize for." Ryland's hand brushes softly over my hair. "This isn't on you. It's on me."

I pull back, wiping my hands across my tear-soaked cheeks.

"How is this on you?"

"I'm the one that knew better. I knew he would never be okay with this and yet I fooled myself into believing that he would."

"I don't care." I take his hands in mine. "I don't care if he never accepts us. I still want to be with you."

"My sweet Ainsley." He releases one of my hands and cups my cheek. "I can't let you sacrifice the only family you have left for me."

"You're my family, too," I argue.

"He's your brother. And he's given up a lot to give you a good life. I can't be the one that gets in the way of that. You both mean too much to me for that."

"What are you saying? That because of Finn we can't be together?"

"I'm saying you should go home. I'm saying you should talk to Finn. I'm saying let's give things a little time to cool off before we figure out how to proceed."

"How to proceed?" I draw back, pushing his hand away. "I just went toe to toe with my brother for you. I just broke his heart. For you.

Because I thought we were on the same page. And now you're telling me that we aren't."

"That's not what I'm saying, Ains. I'm just saying, maybe we should take a step back. At least for now. You have to make this right with Finn."

"Do not tell me what I have to do. Finn will come around or he won't. All I want is to be with you." Emotion clogs my voice.

"I want to be with you, too." His voice is soft and yet there's an edge of apology to it that tells me he's not done. "But I can't be with you knowing that it will take away the only family you have left."

"You talk as though Finn would actually write me off. We both know he won't. He's just mad right now. He'll come around eventually," I insist, panic rising in my throat.

"And if he doesn't?" His gaze drops to the floor.

"He will." I tip his chin back up, forcing him to meet my eyes. "He will."

"I know you want to believe that, but the truth is you can't know for sure. Go home, Ainsley. Talk to your brother."

"And what about you? I'm just supposed to leave you here with no one and nowhere to go?"

"I'm a grown man. I'll figure something out."

"I'm not leaving you."

"Yes, you are."

"You said you wanted this. That you wanted us," I croak, desperation clawing at my chest.

"I do." He steps forward, his hands resting on either side of my face. "Which is why I need you to do this for me. Please." He drops his forehead to mine.

"Ryland."

"Please, Ainsley. Go home."

"I love you," I whisper, fresh tears brewing behind my eyes.

He drops his hold on me before stepping around my car, pulling the door open moments later without uttering a single word. My heart feels like it's about to cave in on itself at any moment.

I don't want to leave. The last thing I want to do is go, but I also know I can't stay.

Without another word, I sink into the driver's seat and fire the engine to life. Ryland is still standing in the same spot as I back out of the garage and reluctantly drive away.

It takes me less than five minutes to pull into the driveway of my house. To my surprise, Finn's car is out front. I half expected him not to come home after the blowout we just had.

Shoving the car into park, I kill the engine and quickly make my way inside. The living room is dark when I enter but the kitchen light is on so I head in that direction.

I locate Finn immediately. He's sitting at the table, a rocks glass and an opened bottle of whiskey in front of him.

He lifts the glass to his lips and throws back the contents when he sees me enter, instantly moving to refill the glass.

"What the fuck are you doing here? Shouldn't you be somewhere consoling your *boyfriend*?" His lips curl around the word like it's painful for him to say.

"Finn." I hesitantly step further into the kitchen. "You have to know, Ryland and I never set out to hurt you. If anything, this is my fault. He wanted to tell you weeks ago."

"*Weeks*?" His wide eyes sweep upward to mine. "This has been going on for weeks?"

"Around the same time you and Lily started dating," I admit, knotting my hands in front of myself.

"Well, you two are damn good liars. I'll give you that." He knocks back the second glass of whiskey and fills a third.

"We weren't lying… Exactly."

"Lying by omission is still lying, Ainsley," he scolds, hurt and anger evident in his eyes.

"I know. I know that. And I know we should have come to you from the very beginning but I was afraid."

"Afraid of what?"

"That you wouldn't be okay with it."

"That should have been your first indication that what you were doing was wrong."

"But it wasn't wrong. In fact, nothing has ever felt more right. But I knew that if you were against it, Ryland would never go along with it. So I convinced him to stay quiet. I needed time to show him that he could love me the way I've always loved him. I just needed time to do it before you messed it all up."

"You know the most fucked up part?" Finn cuts in like he didn't hear a word I said. "I keep replaying all the times I left you with him when you were younger. Hell, he'd sleep over here when you were fourteen and fifteen. Fuck, he slept in your room. I never in a million years thought I had anything to worry about."

"You didn't. Ryland never once made a move on me back then. He never once did anything that would suggest his affection for me was anything more than brotherly. *Ever*. I promise you that. But Finn, look at me. I'm not a little girl anymore. I'm a grown woman. And I started this, not him."

"Do you honestly expect me to believe a single word that comes out of your mouth right now?"

"It doesn't matter what you believe because everything I'm saying is true."

"I raised you to be a lot of things, Ainsley, but a liar wasn't one of them."

"Finn," Lily calls through the house right as the front door opens and closes.

"In the kitchen," he calls out, knocking back his third glass of whiskey in less than five minutes.

Moments later, Lily steps into the kitchen, freezing when she catches sight of my red, tear stained face.

"Um," she hesitates. "Should I come back later?" she asks, looking toward Finn.

"No. You should hear this, too. Seems my little sister and my best friend have been fucking behind my back for weeks." He pours another glass of whiskey as Lily's uncertain expression swings in my direction.

"He's being ridiculous. You should go," I tell her, not wanting Lily to get caught in the crossfire. Especially considering we're already on shaky ground after the way I behaved toward her yesterday.

"No, you shouldn't." Finn stands, the amber liquid sloshing over the edges of his glass as he does. "After dealing with liars all day, I need someone who actually knows how to tell the truth."

"Actually." Lily clears her throat, stopping Finn before he can take more than a step toward her. "I knew about Ryland and Ainsley."

If looks could kill, Lily and I would both be bleeding out on the floor right now.

"What?" He pales, his sole focus on Lily. "Why would you keep this from me?"

"Because it wasn't my place to tell you," she explains simply. "Just because you and I started seeing each other doesn't mean I suddenly have no loyalty to a person who's been my best friend for years."

"I should have known," Finn spits, his anger now mixing with the alcohol, making a lethal combination. "You're just like the fucking rest of them."

"If that's so, then what does that make you, Finn?" she challenges, stepping up next to me.

"What the fuck are you talking about?" He grinds his back molars in annoyance.

"You know exactly what I'm talking about. If tonight is the night that we lay everything on the table, then I think you owe Ainsley the truth, too."

"What is she talking about, Finn?" My eyes dance between Lily and Finn.

"Ainsley's right. You should leave." He throws back the whiskey before slamming the empty glass on the table.

"No, she should stay. What is she talking about, Finn?" I stare at him expectantly, my chest tight with anticipation.

"She doesn't know anything." He gives her a look, one that I can say I've never seen before. A look that makes me afraid for my friend. Not physically but for what this might mean for her relationship. A relationship that I know she's happy in.

"Ainsley." She turns toward me, but I hold my hand up to stop her. As much as I want to know what she has to say, I can't let her be the one to tell me. I can't have her throw away what she has with Finn to tell me something that he clearly needs to be the one to say.

"Don't." I shake my head, trying to convey everything I'm thinking in one brief look. "There's no reason for you to get caught up in this. This is between me and my brother." I tilt my head toward the front of the house. "Just go."

Lily gives me an apologetic look and takes a step back, her face turning toward Finn. "Okay. I'm leaving." With that, she spins around and quickly exits the room.

Finn and I stand in heated silence as we listen to Lily's footstep grow more distant, the front door finally opening before snapping shut behind her.

"What was she talking about?" I ask, my voice eerily calm.

"It's really none of your business."

"No? Because from the way she acted, I'm pretty sure it has something to do with me." I drop my hands to my hips. "Here you are, chastising me for keeping the truth from you when clearly there's something you've been keeping from me. And I want to know what it is."

"Well too fucking bad." He kicks his foot to the side, sending the kitchen chair next to him skidding across the floor.

"You always do that. You expect me to be an open book. You expect me to do everything *you* want me to do. You expect to know all. And yet, you don't tell me anything. We used to talk. I used to feel like I knew you. But since Ryland's been home, you haven't been the same with me. You've shut me out. I can feel it."

"Pretty sure you're the one that shut me out."

"No I didn't. I kept one thing from you."

"You, my best friend, and apparently my girlfriend were all in on it," he sneers.

"Don't be mad at Lily. She never agreed with me on keeping this from you."

"And yet she still lied to me," he fires back.

"To protect me. Her best friend. Or have you forgotten that part?" I square my shoulders. "You moved in on Lily without any regard for me. And yet here you stand on your high horse acting like I did something wrong."

"Again, I never kept Lily from you."

"True. But you also didn't ask me how I would feel about you sleeping with my best friend before you did it. You just did what you wanted. You had no idea how I'd feel. How is that any different? Other than the fact that Ryland and I kept our relationship quiet for a few weeks?" I add at the end, knowing that's going to be his argument.

"We've been over this. The differences between me and Lily, and you and Ryland, are incomparable. Stop trying to use that as your justification for what you've done."

"I don't have to justify anything to you. I'm an adult who is free to make my own choices. But because I love you and I care about our relationship, I'm trying to explain."

"I don't need *your* version of an explanation. What I need is for you to stop fucking Ryland."

"God!" I throw my hands up in the air. "Is that really all you think we were doing? That we were just fucking? We were building a relationship for Christ's sake. We were spending time together and getting to know each other again."

"I don't give a fuck what you were doing. It ends now." He snags the whiskey bottle off the table and lifts it to his lips, bypassing the glass completely this time.

"That's not your call." I try to keep my voice as even as I can.

"Actually, it is. That is, if you want to continue to live here."

"Are you threatening to kick me out?" I draw back.

"End things with Ryland or you are no longer welcome in this house."

I stand stunned for several seconds, tears blurring my vision.

"You know what, I don't want to be here with you anymore anyways." With that, I spin around and quickly walk away.

Chapter 22

Ryland

"What the fuck are you doing here?" Finn's gaze narrows when he opens the front door to find me standing on the porch.

"I know I'm the last person you want to see right now," I start, not getting the opportunity to finish before Finn cuts me off.

"Pretty fucking observant," he grunts.

"I would have asked if it was okay if I stop by had you shown up for work today. I just need to get some clothes. Five minutes. That's all I need."

"Tell my sister to come home and you can have your shit."

"What?" I'm momentarily caught off guard by his words. "Ainsley isn't here?"

"Don't fucking play that game with me. I know she went to you after she left here last night."

"No, Finn." I shake my head. "I haven't seen her since I sent her away after you left."

"You sent her away?" He gives me a doubtful look.

"I told her she needed to make things right with you. I assumed she came back here to talk to you."

"Oh she did. And then she left again."

"Where did she go?"

"Fuck if I know. I assumed she was with you."

"I crashed on the couch in Jim's office. She never came back there. Maybe she's with Lily."

"Probably." He hesitates before stepping out of the doorway. "You have five minutes." I can tell by the look on his face that the last thing he wants to do is let me in but for some reason he does anyway.

"I'll be in and out before you know it," I promise, sliding past him before immediately heading toward my bedroom. Or, what used to be my bedroom.

Stepping inside, I flip on the lights and head for the closet, snagging my duffle bag off the floor before proceeding to shove handfuls of clothes inside of it. I don't bother to fold them. I don't doubt that Finn will have my ass out the door at five minutes on the dot, so I need to focus on getting as much shit as I can before that happens.

As much as I want to try to hash all this out with him, I also don't want to further intensify the rift between us. He has to do this his way.

I get where he's coming from. I really do. Ainsley is his little sister. He gave up so much for her. But I also gave up a lot for her. More than she will ever know. The fact that he seems to have forgotten this, that what I did for both of them has been so easily swept under the rug, is a very fucking hard pill to swallow. But I can't start throwing stones if I hope to salvage even a shred of this friendship.

I did what I did because I knew it was right. I'd do it again tomorrow if it came down to it. Even with things being as fucked up as they are right now, I'd do everything in my power to protect this family.

Ainsley's face flashes through my mind. Her tear-filled eyes, the uncertainty in her expression as she climbed into her car and drove away last night. It nearly fucking broke me. Because even though I said we'd see how all this plays out, deep down I knew I was letting her go.

Ainsley doesn't belong to me. She never has. I was foolish to let myself believe that I could have her. And now I've fucked up both of our lives because I refused to see things for how they are instead of how I want them to be.

But even knowing all this, even knowing that there's no way we can be together, it doesn't mean I don't want to be with her. Because I do. I want to fight for her with everything that I have. I want to show her and the rest of the world just how much she means to me. But if doing so means she loses Finn, I could never live with myself. And I think he's made it pretty clear where he stands on the matter.

Once I have as much packed into my duffle as it can carry, I head back out into the living room. I pass by Finn who's sitting on the couch without a word, making a beeline for the front door.

I grab the knob then hesitate, knowing there's no way I can leave shit the way it is. Even if it fixes nothing, I have to at least try to apologize to him.

I turn toward Finn, his focus on the television in front of him, even though I know he's not actually paying any attention to what's on. Last time I checked, he had zero interest in baseball.

"For what it's worth, I'm really sorry about all of this," I say, letting out a slow breath. "I know it doesn't count for much, but I at least wanted you to know that."

When I get no reaction from him, I hoist my duffle higher on my shoulder and turn back to the door, tugging it open.

"Do you love her?" His voice stops me dead in my tracks. I turn back to find him sitting in the same position, his gaze still locked on the television.

"What?" I question, truthfully not sure how to answer him.

"Ainsley. Do you love her?" he asks again. "I mean, do you actually love her?"

"I do." I ignore my initial gut instinct to lie and decide that it's time I'm honest, and not just with Finn but with myself as well.

Finn slowly pushes to his feet and turns toward me. "Because she clearly loves you, and that's not easy for me to admit."

"You have to know, I never wanted anything to go down this way. I didn't mean for any of it to happen and I sure as fuck didn't mean to fall in love with her. But I did, man. I fell so fucking hard from so high up that I'm pretty sure I still haven't hit the ground." Despite the heaviness of the situation, a trace of a smile graces my lips.

"I gave her an ultimatum." He shuffles his feet. "I told her she either ended things with you or she was no longer welcome here," he admits, regret the most prominent emotion on his face. "She left. Without a single fucking belonging. She just turned around and walked out. I was so sure I could force her to see things my way that I never considered she'd push back."

"Of course she pushed back. She's Ainsley. She's *your* sister. You taught her to stand on her own two feet and fight for what she wants."

"As much as I wanted her to concede and let me have my way, a part of me is glad she didn't." He pauses. "I've done everything for that girl. I gave up my life, my future, to make sure she had one. I abandoned every dream I had of getting out of this hell hole, and it was never a question. It wasn't *am I going to do this*, I knew I had to. And not for any reason other than she's my fucking sister and if I have one job on this earth." He holds up his index finger. "Just one job. It's to protect her."

"You know I would die for her just like you would. I get why you're pissed, Finn. If the roles we're reversed you'd probably look a hell of a lot worse than I do right now." I gesture to my face that's got a pretty good gash under my eye and a very prominent bruise on my cheek. "But you have to see that there isn't a thing I wouldn't do for that girl. For both of you. I think after everything I've proven that much to you."

"I want more for her than you can give her," he tells me honestly. "It may be my fault, but you're an ex-con, Ryland. You'll be an ex-con for the rest of your life. That stigma will follow you everywhere you go. Maybe that's adequate for this life," he gestures around the room, "but not for the life she deserves."

"I may not be able to get a job that would allow me to give her the finer things in life, but when have you ever known Ainsley to want those things?"

"You haven't been around for the last five years. You haven't listened to her talk about how she can't wait to graduate college so she can get a good job and a place of her own, far away from this shit hole. She wants out, man. And if she's with you, she'll be stuck here forever."

His words are like a knife to my chest. I know they're true, but it doesn't make hearing them any less painful.

"I don't know how to make this right," I admit after a long moment of silence has passed between us. "Either way, I lose."

"I'm not okay with what went down," Finn interjects. "And it's going to take me some time to feel like I can trust you again. But after having some time to think about it, I get how it happened. You and Ainsley have always shared this weird connection. When she was little, she'd always ask for you before me. As she got older, that didn't change. You were the one who slept on her floor when she had nightmares. You were the one consoling her after dad died. You were the one who made sure she was still able to find happiness in spite of everything bad going on in her life. You took her to the park and the movies. You two did everything together. And when you got locked up, it nearly fucking killed her. And I was the one that had to sit here and watch it. I had to watch her go from adoring you, to missing you, to hating you. I watched her affection morph into anger and I couldn't do anything to make it better. She loved you even then. I just didn't want to admit it to myself because doing so meant that I made the wrong choice in letting you take the fall. Because I think she'd have been better off with you all along."

"Finn, we both know that isn't true. She needed you. She still does."

He shakes his head. "She doesn't need me. Not anymore. Maybe not ever. It's always been you. I think in a way I've always known it. I've always been jealous of the bond you had with her. We may be close, but we were never as close as you two were. No matter what I did, she always chose you. Hell, she's still choosing you."

"You have done more for her than any brother should have to."

"Yeah, but how great of a brother could I really be if I let the one person she loved more than anyone else take the fall for something I did?"

"Finn, we've been over this. I did what I did because that's what families do for each other.

There's no way a judge would have given me guardianship of her had you gone to prison. My family was an absolute shit show and I had no way to support a fifteen-year-old. Ainsley would have ended up in the system and neither of us wanted that to happen."

"I feel like this is my punishment. That this is what I get for letting you go to prison."

"You have to be joking, right?" I drop my duffle next to the door and take a step back into the room. "This is on me. This has nothing to do with what went down five years ago. I broke your trust. I took advantage of a girl that deserved better from me. And I lied and covered it up because I knew deep down how fucked up it all was. The best thing I could have done for her, and for you, was head in the opposite direction the second those prison doors opened."

"That's not true and you know it." Finn shakes his head.

"I went to prison for five years to protect her and then I came back here and ruined everything for her."

"Ryland?" I turn toward the soft voice, paralyzed when I see Ainsley standing in the doorway of the kitchen.

Chapter 23

Ainsley

My heart feels like it's about to beat straight out of my chest as my gaze slides back and forth between Ryland and Finn. *I went to prison for five years to protect her...* Ryland's words sound over and over again in my head as I stand here trying to process what they mean.

"Ainsley." Finn takes a step toward me but I hold up a hand to stop him. What Lily said about Finn keeping something from me last night comes to the forefront of my mind.

"What did you mean?" I turn toward Ryland. "What did you mean when you said you went to prison to protect me?"

"I'm not sure what all you heard, but I can explain." Ryland holds his hands up in front of himself and takes a hesitant step forward like I'm some wild animal that may pounce at any moment.

"No, it's me who needs to explain," Finn speaks up, pulling both mine and Ryland's attention to him. "I was so angry with you for lying to me about you and Ryland," he says, his eyes locked on mine. "That I never stopped to wonder why I was so angry. But then I realized, it's not you I was angry with. It's myself. Because I've been lying to you, too… For the last five years."

"Finn," Ryland interjects.

"Don't." Finn shakes his head at him. "She needs to know the truth. It's time that everything was out in the open."

"The truth about what?" I butt in, starting to lose my patience.

"Ryland wasn't the one selling drugs the night we were arrested," Finn says after what feels like an eternity. "I was."

"Wait… What…" I stutter, not able to string together a single set of words. "Is it true?" I finally find my voice, my gaze sliding to Ryland before going back to my brother. "Ryland took the fall for you?"

Finn drops his head. "It's true."

"All this time. All these years. You let me hate him. You let me believe that he had abandoned me. And all the while he was covering for you?" My voice breaks at the end.

"I had never dealt with any drugs before that. I came across an opportunity to make a quick buck and I took it. We needed the money and truthfully I thought it would be easy. Take the drugs to the drop off, switch out the money, and drive away. I'd make a few hundred dollars and no one would be any the wiser."

"Then explain to me how your best friend spent five years in prison?" My knees shake under my weight.

"Ryland was with me. He had no idea what I was doing. I told him I needed to drop off something to a friend. When he questioned me on it, I had to come clean. He knew me well enough to know I was lying. Once he learned what I was doing, he insisted on doing the drop for me, just in case anything went down. Knowing I was now your legal guardian and what would happen to you if, on the off chance, things went sideways, I decided to let him. When he dropped the package, the guy whipped out his badge. I thought it was all over, that we were both going down. But Ryland told the cops it was all him. He insisted that I had no idea what was in the bag. When we were in the back of the cop car he made me promise not to tell anyone the truth. I didn't want to let him take the fall, but he reminded me what would happen to you if the cops learned that I was involved. He sacrificed himself... For you. I guess that should have been my first indication of how much you actually mean to him."

He looks over at Ryland, an apologetic look passing over his face.

"You let me believe the worst," I say, more to myself than to anyone else.

"I asked him not to tell you. I thought it would be easier," Ryland says.

"Easier for who?" I ask, my voice shaking. "I get not telling the cops." I turn back to Finn. "I understand why you thought you were doing the right thing. But Finn, you let me hate him for five years. You let me blame him. All the while you could have told me the truth."

"I could stand here and lie to you, tell you that I only wanted to honor what Ryland had asked of me. But the truth is, that wasn't the only reason I didn't tell you. I was afraid of what you would think of me if you knew the truth. I've never told anyone. Well, except Lily, and that was a guilty confession after a night of having too much to drink."

"All this time." I shake my head. "All this time and you continued to breathe life into the lie. And then to react the way you did last night. After everything that man has done for you. How dare you!" I point my finger at him.

"I'm not innocent in this, I'll admit that. But what you two did stands on its own. Ryland and I came to an agreement. One that kept you safe and at home with me. But him sleeping with you," Finn shakes his head, "that crosses a line I can't look past."

"And that's your problem, Finn. It's always about you. What you can live with. What you can or can't accept. God! We didn't do this to hurt you. In fact, this had nothing to do with you. But even after everything he did for you, after everything he did for me, you can't see what he means to me. What he's always meant to me. Ryland is more to this family than just your best friend. He's also the person I'm in love with. And yet for some reason you continue to deny me of the one thing that makes my life worth anything. And not just now, but you've been doing it for the last five years."

"Ainsley, that's not fair. You act like I purposely set out to make you miserable. All I ever wanted was for you to be happy, to be taken care of."

"You gave up a lot to give me a good and happy home after dad died, I know that. You weren't perfect, but you did the best you could. And I will forever be grateful for everything you did for me. But this, what you did to Ryland, what you're still doing to him. You are so far from the person I thought you were. I thought you were the most selfless person I know. Turns out you're more selfish than any of us." I turn, not able to stand here and look at him for a moment longer.

"Ainsley, please. I'm sorry." His voice is riddled in defeat.

"Yeah, Finn, so am I."

"Ainsley." Ryland tries to stop me as I head for the door.

"Don't." I shake him off. "Just because he's the hypocrite doesn't mean you didn't lie to me right alongside him. I thought I could trust you. Make that two times now that you've broken that trust. I wouldn't count on there being a third."

I shove past him and quickly exit the house, jogging to the street where my car is parked. I was hoping to sneak in the back, gather a few things, and sneak back out undetected before heading back to Matt's. He shares an off-campus apartment with a couple other students who went home for the summer and was sweet enough to let me crash in one of their rooms last night. But after hearing Ryland and Finn talking, my plan of a quick and easy escape went right out the window.

Quickly starting my car, I've just popped it into gear when a hand slides over my mouth, pulling my head back against the headrest. Seconds later I feel the cold bite of steel against my throat.

Warm breath dances across my cheek as a menacing voice fills the car. "Drive."

Chapter 24

Ryland

"Is she here?" Finn bursts into Jim's office looking primed for a fight.

"What? Who?" I don't try to hide my confusion or the irritation I feel over him barging in without even announcing himself first.

"Don't fucking play with me. Ainsley. Is she here?"

"No," I answer him honestly, gesturing around the office. "I haven't seen her since yesterday."

I didn't stick around after Ainsley took off. Between her running out the way she did and Finn going back and forth between wanting to set things right and wanting to tear my head off, I didn't see a reason to subject myself to further torment.

I said my peace. What happens now isn't really up to me.

"She hasn't come back home." He looks worried. I don't know how I didn't see it before now. "You haven't seen her?"

"No. I haven't heard a word out of her. Then again, I didn't expect to after the fucking bomb we dropped on her yesterday." I grind my teeth. "Have you checked with Lily?"

"Have I checked with Lily?" He gives me a look that says I should know him better than that. "Of course I fucking checked with Lily. She's the first person I called after her boss contacted me to find out why Ainsley didn't show up for work this afternoon."

This gets my attention and I immediately go rigid. I may have been absent for the last five years, but I've been home long enough to know how crazy Ainsley is about her routine. She never misses school or work unless absolutely necessary, and I know for a fact she isn't the type to not at least call if she isn't going to be somewhere.

Worry pools in my gut.

"You think something's wrong?" I ask Finn, my voice tight.

"I don't know. I'm trying not to jump to a worst case scenario but I can't find her. She's not with Lily. She's not at any of her usual hang out spots. And her phone goes straight to voicemail."

"Maybe she's with another friend. Maybe she needed some time alone, away from everyone." I try to think this through rationally and keep my composure, even though internally I'm starting to panic a little.

"So she just decides to pull a no call no show at work?" He gives me an incredulous look.

"We both know that's not something Ainsley would do."

"So what the fuck do we do?" I ask, a sick feeling turning in my stomach.

"We widen the search. I'll call Lily, have her call around to some of Ainsley's other friends and co-workers. I'm going to drive around, see if I can find her car." He runs a hand through his hair. "You head to the house in case she shows up there."

I nod in agreement, standing to clasp his shoulder. "We'll find her. I swear it," I promise him, knowing we don't have a choice. There is no other option. Neither of us will rest until she's been located safe and sound.

He gives me a stiff nod before turning and taking off out of the office with me fast on his heels.

"Hey, Lil, anything?" I stop pacing and set my gaze on Lily as she ends the call she was on and heads up the front steps of the porch where both Finn and I are standing. The look on her face only adds to my uneasiness.

It's been hours. We've been everywhere. Up and down every street. Knocking on doors, talking to neighbors. Lily has called everyone she can think of. There hasn't been any sign of Ainsley.

It's nearing ten o'clock now. It's been nearly twenty-eight hours since anyone has seen Ainsley. The more time that passes, the more restless I become. I'm trying so hard to remain positive, but I find my optimism waning with each minute that ticks by with no word.

"That was Matt. He was at work and just got my messages. Apparently, Ainsley stayed at his place Friday night after she left here. He said she left yesterday evening to come home and get some clothes with the intention of returning, but she never came back. Matt said he tried to call her a few times but figured something happened to change her mind about coming back. He assumed he would hear from her later."

"Fuck," I draw out, having hoped that when Matt finally called her back we'd know more than we did before. Unfortunately, all we've learned is where she was Friday night.

"We have to be missing something." Finn shakes his head. "Can you think of anyone else? Anyone she's had any contact with recently? Anyone we're not thinking of?"

"Well, I have one more person I could call, but it's not likely he'll be very helpful. He and Ainsley aren't exactly on good terms."

"Who?" Finn asks.

"Oscar."

"The baseball player Oscar? The one Ainsley dated in high school. I thought he was off to college in another state."

"He's home for the summer," I interject. "Ainsley and I ran into him when we were leaving the movies a couple weeks back. Intense dude."

"Intense doesn't even begin to cover it." Lily's brow furrows.

"What?" Finn questions. "What are you not telling us?"

"Let's just figure out where he lives and talk to him." Lily brushes Finn's questions off. "Let me make another call." With that, she spins around and heads back down the steps.

I watch with bated breath as she paces the front yard, her cell phone pressed to her ear. She's on the call for less than two minutes before she announces that she has an address.

"Ryland and I will go check it out. You wait here in case Ainsley shows up."

"Absolutely not," Lily argues. "I'm not going to sit here going out of my mind with worry. I have to do something. Besides, I know more about Oscar than either of you. And, I think he'll be more likely to talk to me than either of you. We can leave a note on the door for Ainsley to call us if she comes home."

Finn mulls it over for a few seconds before agreeing to Lily's demands. She jots a quick note and tapes it inside the screen door before joining Finn and me in the car.

We don't have to GPS the address. Turns out Oscar lives a few blocks away, and given that Finn and I grew up in the neighborhood, it's an area we know well.

When we pull up outside of the small brick ranch, Finn and I both turn back to Lily who's sitting in the backseat.

"You two stay here," she tells us, climbing out of the car before either of us have a chance to respond.

The car is eerily quiet as we watch Lily approach the house. It's late, but there appears to be lights on inside so I'm hopeful that someone is home and awake.

From where we are on the street we have the perfect view of the front door, so when a middle-aged woman answers, we are able to watch the exchange. Unfortunately the woman is the only person Lily talks to before she turns around and heads back to the car after a few short moments.

"Anything?" Finn and I both ask in unison as Lily climbs back into the backseat.

"That was Oscar's mom. She hasn't heard from him since yesterday."

"That can't be a coincidence, can it?" Finn asks, his gaze darting to me.

"No, I don't think it is," Lily interjects. "Apparently, Oscar has been lying as well. His mom was confused when I mentioned that I knew Oscar was home for the summer. According to her, he's been home for months. Something to do with his baseball scholarship. Yet when Ainsley ran into him at the end of May, he told her he was in town for a baseball tournament. Given what his mom just told me, that was a lie."

"What are you getting at? Do you think Oscar might know where Ainsley is?" I cut her off.

"You met the guy." She narrows her gaze at me. "I don't think he just knows where she is. I think he's involved somehow."

"What the fuck are you talking about?" Finn turns all the way around in his seat to be able to see Lily.

"There's more to Oscar and Ainsley's relationship than you know about." She kneads her bottom lip between her teeth. "I wasn't friends with her when they dated, but apparently a little while into their relationship he started to become really controlling. Like, wouldn't let Ainsley even talk to another guy without going into a jealous rage. It got bad enough that she eventually ended things with him. He stalked her for a while after that and things got physical a couple of times. He would show up where she was and make some random excuse for being there. Ainsley was scared of him. And even before he supposedly came back, Ainsley had expressed some concern to me on a couple different occasions that she felt like she was being watched. Just last week she said something. I thought it was her still being a little freaked out over the break-in, but now I'm wondering if maybe someone really was watching her. I mean, if Oscar's been in town this whole time, it would make sense, right?"

"So you're telling me that a guy who used to date my sister, a guy she was afraid of, has been lying to everyone about where he's been and now he's missing and so is my sister?"

Lily swallows hard and nods.

"And you didn't think to mention any of this sooner?" he bites, fear and anger lacing his voice. "You didn't think that maybe mentioning that my sister had some crazed stalker following her around might have been information we needed to know?"

"I didn't even think about it. I was thinking she was probably with one of her friends or something. I never considered that she could be in actual real danger."

"So what the fuck do we do now?" I intervene. "How do we find him?"

"I asked his mom if she knew where he might be. She said he spends a lot of time at his grandpa's fishing cabin off of Old Mill Road."

Finn and I exchange a brief look before he's facing forward again, forcing the car into drive.

"Did you get an address?"

"I did." She rambles off the house number.

With that, Finn punches the gas.

Chapter 25

Ainsley

My head bobs forward, jolting me from sleep right as exhaustion starts to take me under. I can't fall asleep. No matter how badly I want to. No matter how badly my body screams for it. I have to stay awake.

I force my eyes open and slowly lift my head, scanning the room for the thousandth time since I've been locked in here. I have no idea how much time has passed. I don't even know if it's night or day.

My mouth is so dry the corners of my lips have started to crack and I'm fairly certain I've lost circulation in both of my hands from the position they're tied in. I can barely feel my fingers at all.

When I ran out of my house, all I could think about was how the two people that mean the most to me had been lying to me for years. It seemed unforgivable at the time. Now, it seems so ridiculous that I would be laughing at myself if I wasn't in so much pain.

It's funny how one moment things seem life or death and the next you realize what life or death really means. Because truthfully, right now, death seems like a very real possibility. I haven't eaten or had even a sip of water since I arrived here. I wish I knew how long ago that had been. I wish I knew what was happening. I wish I knew *why* this was happening.

I have no idea where I am. Only that I was forced to drive out to Old Mill Road before pulling my car into an abandoned barn. After that, I was blindfolded and traipsed through a heavily wooded area for a couple of miles. I could tell because I could see the path through the bottom of my blindfold and could feel the branches and shrubs scratch my arms as the foliage became thicker.

One thing I do know is *who* brought me here.

Oscar…

He may have worn a mask and tried to disguise his voice, but I wasn't fooled. I'd recognize him anywhere. The gritty rasp in his tone that's impossible to cover up. The scar on the back of his right hand that he got when he wrecked his scooter as a kid. The smell of his cologne.

I spent months of my life loving that smell. Now it makes me sick to my stomach.

He may think he's smart, but I know it's him. I know it without a single doubt. The only real question now is what he plans to do with me now that he's got me here.

Ryland's face flashes through my mind.

Does he even know I'm missing?

Is he out looking for me?

Has he noticed I'm gone?

These are the thoughts that have plagued me over the last several hours. But also the thoughts that have given me a semblance of hope. Because if he knows I'm missing, if Finn knows, that means they're looking for me.

I jump when the door at the top of the stairs swings open. Each clunky footstep makes my pulse spike higher and higher until I feel like there's no way my heart could possibly beat any faster.

When Oscar comes into view about halfway down the staircase, I have to resist the urge to scream for help. It's a natural reaction, but one that won't get me anywhere. I've tried over and over again and all it's done is to further irritate my already raw throat.

"Oscar," I practically whimper when he steps in front of me.

At least now he has the balls to show his face.

To the blind eye, Oscar looks like every other good-looking all-American guy. He's perfected the act. The do gooder. The scholar. The athlete. The dream son. But who he shows the world is not the person he actually is. I've learned this the hard way.

"How it pains me to see you like this." Oscar runs the tip of his index finger down the side of my face, making every inch of my skin crawl.

"Please, Oscar. Please let me go. I'll give you anything you want. Anything. Please. Just let me go."

"I gave you the opportunity to give me what I wanted." He crouches down so that he's eye level with me. "Instead, you chose to give it to someone else. Ryland, is it?" A wicked smile curls his mouth as he reaches behind him and pulls something from the back pocket of his jeans.

He waves the folded knife in front of my face, making a spectacle of the whole thing. And even though the last thing I want to do is react, I can't help but jump when he hits a button on the side and the knife pops open, revealing a thick, at least six-inch-long, serrated blade.

"Yes. Ryland," he continues, sliding the smooth side of the blade down my neck. "He seems quite taken with you. Not that I can blame him. Wonder how much he'll miss you now that you're gone."

He slides the knife lower, stopping right above my collar bone, before pressing the serrated side of the blade into my flesh. I start to cry when it pricks my skin. I can't help it. Tears flood my vision and my entire body starts to tremble in fear.

This is it. This is how I'm going to die. At the hands of a man I once trusted. At the hands of the person I gave my virginity to. Locked in a dark, dingy basement where no one can find me. With no way to make things right with Ryland or my brother. No chance to say I'm sorry or goodbye.

"Don't worry." He laughs, the sound dark and demented. "I won't hurt you unless you make me." He retracts the knife from my skin before sliding it lower, slicing open the front of my shirt to reveal my bra covered chest. "Mmm." He hums before I feel his tongue slide across the top of my breast.

I cringe at the contact, thinking I'd almost rather have the knife there than his mouth.

"Oscar. Why are you doing this?" I plead with him when he pulls back and looks at me, a shadow of the person I once felt like I knew.

"Why?" His smile fades. "You know why."

"But I don't. I have no idea what I could have done for you to do this to me."

"You know, I tried being the good guy. The guy I thought you wanted me to be. But then you pushed me, Ainsley. You pushed me too far. I had to have you and I wasn't going to share you with anyone else."

"But you left," I point out. "You've been gone for over two years."

"You're right. I did leave. I tried to forget you. I tried to purge you from my system. But nothing worked. I couldn't stay away. I kept coming back. Over and over I came back. I had to see you, even if you didn't know I was there." The way he says it makes my entire body quiver. "But every time I left it became harder to stay away. My grades slipped. I couldn't concentrate on the field. I was under your spell and it cost me everything."

"Oscar."

"You." He holds the tip of the blade directly under my chin, forcing me to keep my face level with his. "You cost me my scholarship. You cost me my future. And now you are all I have."

"I didn't do anything," I whimper, too afraid to even attempt to move.

"You were a good girl," he continues as if I didn't even speak. "You were a very good girl. But then *he* showed up. He showed up and touched what is mine. *You* are mine, Ainsley. You've always been mine. From the moment I first tasted you. From the moment you gave me what no other man had touched, I knew you'd be mine forever." He leans in so close I can feel his breath on my face. "But then I saw you with *him*. I saw you share what was mine. You let him touch you. You let him inside of you." He runs his nose along my cheek, inhaling deeply as he does. "You let him have what is mine." He pulls back a couple of inches.

"Oscar, please."

"Oscar, please." He mocks me. "You know, I came to your house to surprise you. I came there thinking you'd be happy to see me. Only you weren't alone," he hisses. "So, I took some mementos, though I must say I was disappointed you had just done laundry. I prefer the smell of your pussy over detergent any day. But alas, I had to make do with what I could get my hands on. I knew you'd want me to have them."

"It was you. You were the one who broke into my house."

"Broke in?" he balks. "I prefer to look at it as entering without your knowledge. Though I did intend to make my presence known. That was before I realized what a lying, cheating whore you are." His eyes grow darker.

"I didn't lie or cheat on you, Oscar. We aren't together. We haven't been together in years."

"You are mine!" he screams in my face. "You. Are. Mine!" he reiterates, stopping after each word to really drive his point home.

I want to argue. I want to tell him that he's a sick, twisted, disgusting human being. That I could never be with someone like him again. But I know that will only further diminish what little chance I have of getting out of here alive.

I don't know if Oscar has it in him to kill me. I don't know if his psychopathic tendencies stop at harassment and abuse or if he's full on deranged. But I do know that I don't want to find out if I can help it.

So instead of fighting back, I try to lull him into a sense of comfort.

"I didn't want him," I tell him. "I never wanted him. I always only ever wanted you. But you left me. I thought you didn't want me anymore."

"You're lying," he snarls.

"I'm not lying. Why would I ever want him? He's a liar. A manipulator. A loser who spent the last five years in jail. He could never give me the life you could. I know that now."

"And yet conveniently you're just now figuring this out?" He tisks at me. "Oh my dear, Ainsley. I'm not nearly as stupid as you think I am."

"I don't think you're stupid."

"And yet you pitch me the most cliché argument there is." He cocks his head to the side. "You should know me better than that by now."

"Oscar, please. What do I have to do? I'll do anything."

"I don't need you to do anything. You see, I'm the one in control here. Not you." He pulls the knife out from under my chin.

I let out a slow breath but I'm sure to keep my gaze locked on him. I'm not foolish enough to look away. He's demanding to be seen and I am in no place to deny his request, he's made sure of that.

"For now, I think I'll indulge a little." He leans down and slides the knife through the rope binding my feet, sawing it away. "Time to christen your new room." He stands, jerking me to my feet. My legs wobble under my weight and I nearly topple over. Even if I attempted to run, I don't think I'd have the strength to make my legs carry me fast enough to get away from him.

Looping an arm around my waist, he leads me to a tiny dank room under the stairs and guides me inside. There's a small twin bed tucked into the corner void of any bedding, the room otherwise empty.

"I hope you like it in here," he tells me, crossing the small space. "I cleaned it out just for you." He shoves me down on top of the mattress moments later, leaving my arms angled awkwardly behind me.

At first I thought maybe this was a whim. Maybe Oscar had too much to drink and took things too far. But I'm starting to realize that he planned this. He planned *all* of it. And it's even worse than

I thought. He didn't bring me here to kill me. He brought me here to *keep* me.

"Oscar, you don't have to do this," I beg as he hovers over me, popping open the button of his jeans. "Just untie my hands. Untie my hands and I'll give you what you want." I try to kick him off of me when he moves to remove my shorts, but it only serves to egg him on.

"Keep kicking and I'll tie your feet to the bed," he warns, ripping the jean material down my legs.

I'm torn between wanting to fight with everything I have and knowing if I do it won't do me a bit of good. My hands are still bound. Hell, I'm not even sure I could get off this bed if I tried. And yet, I know I have to.

"If you behave, I might bring you something to eat and drink after." Oscar straightens seconds before his hand slides between my thighs.

I can't let this happen. Without warning, I kick at Oscar's hand that's holding the knife as hard as I can. It goes flying across the room. Before he has a chance to react, I pull my leg up then extend it into his groin with every ounce of strength I have left.

Oscar howls in pain before dropping to his knees. I roll and kick, somehow managing to get myself off the bed, but I'm not quick enough. Just as I turn to run, Oscar grabs my ankle and given the weakened state of my legs, my knee buckles and I fall to the floor, my shoulder colliding hard with the cold concrete.

I ignore the pain shooting through me as I try to kick out of Oscar's grasp, attempting to claw my way to the door. His energy is split between keeping me in the room and trying to reach the knife at the same time. Which gives me enough of an upper hand. When he extends for the knife, I pull my foot back and the second he turns back toward me, I land a heel straight to his face. I hear the crack of cartilage as my foot collides with his nose. Blood starts spurting everywhere.

Oscar loses his grip on my foot and I'm able to muster enough strength to scramble away.

"You fucking bitch!" he screams as I reach the door.

I don't turn back to see what he's doing or where he is. I have only one thought pumping through every pore in my body… *Run.*

Despite how impossible each step feels to climb, I somehow manage to make it to the top. Only when I reach the door, it's locked.

Panic and fear nearly cripple me, but I can't give up yet. I push on the door with all my might, kicking it and ramming my shoulder into it as hard as I can.

"Did you really think I'd make it that easy for you?" Oscar says from behind me, the sound of his voice causing the little hairs on the back of my neck to stand.

I turn to find him standing at the bottom of the stairs, blood pouring from his nose, soaking his gray t-shirt.

"You know." He waves the knife at me as he steps onto the bottom step. "I wasn't going to hurt you. I was only going to keep you here with me, where we could be together forever." He smiles. "But now. When I'm done with you you're going to beg for death."

"I'd rather die than be stuck here with you!" I scream.

"If that's what you want." He stops two steps below me, holding the knife in a way that if I try to kick he can easily stab or cut me to stop my advance.

"What I want is for you to let me go." My voice shakes, my adrenaline running so high I feel like my body might split apart at any moment.

I twist my hands, the rope biting into my wrist with every move I make.

"We both know that isn't going to happen." He lifts his leg to climb another step and I know it's now or never.

Even if I die, I'd rather die than give him any part of me. Without a second thought, I lunge at him. He's able to get the knife up just in time that it rips into my stomach as we both go tumbling down the stairs.

His weight crashes over me as we roll. My arm snaps behind me, sending a blinding pain through my body. The blade slices deeper into my abdomen and I gasp for air. And then my head collides with the concrete floor seconds before everything fades to black.

Chapter 26

Ryland

I've never been scared of anything. Not my stepdad. Not prison. Not anything.

That is until last night.

Walking down those stairs to find Ainsley unconscious and bleeding, I felt a fear like I had never known. A paralyzing fear. One that sliced me straight to my core.

We were too late…

In that moment I truly believed she was dead.

But then I got closer and I saw her chest moving. It was shallow and labored, but she was breathing. And once again I had hope.

I didn't know how bad her injuries were, only that she wouldn't wake up. Her arms were bound behind her. She was bleeding from her stomach and her head. She looked so pale and lifeless that I was afraid to touch her.

It didn't take long to confirm it was Oscar laying beneath her. Even with his busted nose and blood covered face, I recognized him instantly.

And he was dead.

The paramedics called it when they arrived on scene. He's lucky the fall down the stairs broke his neck because had I gotten my hands on him first, his death would have been slow and so painful he would have been begging me to end it.

"How's our girl?" I look up when Finn enters the hospital room, two cups of coffee in his hand.

"No change," I tell him, shifting in the uncomfortable chair next to Ainsley's bed.

"Here." He extends one cup to me. "The doctor said it could take hours for her to wake up, maybe even days," he reminds me.

Like I need the reminder. I hung onto every word the doctor said like a lifeline, because I need something to cling to. Some sort of hope.

It's been fourteen hours since we arrived at the hospital. Fourteen long, grueling hours of waiting and hoping.

They'd rushed Ainsley into surgery the moment we arrived. It took them nearly five hours to repair the damage in her abdomen and close the gash in her head, and another two to fix her arm which was shattered so severely they didn't know if they could. Thankfully, they have a skilled orthopedic surgeon on staff that was able to set her arms with pins. The recovery process will be long and painful, and will require future surgeries but at least she's still here. At least she's alive.

Learning that there was no indication of sexual assault was also a huge relief. Considering how we found her, stripped to her underwear with her shirt hanging open.

I shudder to think about what she must have went through down in that basement. How hard she clearly fought.

"I know," I finally respond, lifting the cup to my lips before taking a tentative sip of the hot liquid.

"Have you gotten any sleep at all?" Finn asks, stepping up beside Ainsley's bed to look down at his sister.

"I've dozed a little but not much."

"You really need to try to get some sleep. You're not going to be any good for her when she wakes up if you're walking around like a zombie."

"You're one to talk." I give him a knowing look.

"I slept for a couple of hours this morning." He shrugs, taking a drink of his coffee. He stares down at Ainsley for a long moment before his gaze slides to mine. "I can't stop thinking about all the time we wasted. If we had tried harder. If we had acted faster. Then Ainsley wouldn't be laying in this hospital bed right now."

"Finn, this isn't on you. You were the one that knew something was off. You were the one who called Lily, who came to me. You led the charge that ultimately led us to her."

"And yet I'm the reason she found herself in this mess to begin with." He swallows hard. "Had I not given her an ultimatum, had I supported her when she said she wanted to be with you, she never would have left."

"You're right, maybe Oscar wouldn't have gotten to her when he did. But the fact still remains that he would have. You heard the police. There was evidence in that cabin that he'd been stalking her for months. That he had been planning this for months. None of this is your fault."

"Well it doesn't feel that way to me. I can't help but think about how much I let her down. For fuck's sake, Ryland, I didn't know a thing about the Oscar situation. She told me they broke up and that was that. I had no idea that he stalked her. That he harassed her. That he was so obsessed with her he'd kidnap her. What does that say about me?"

"It says that you were raising a teenage girl. You can't expect that she's going to tell you everything and you can't hold yourself accountable for things happening that were beyond your control."

"I just feel like I failed her on every level."

"You didn't," I argue, pushing to a stand so that we are both standing, facing each other on opposite sides of Ainsley's bed.

"I did." He nods. "And I failed you, too." He blows out a heavy breath through his nose. "You are my family. The one person I know without a second thought that I can count on. Not only did I let you take the fall for something I did, but I tried to stand in the way of you finding happiness once you finally got your life back. I was scared. Of losing her. Of losing you. I felt myself losing control and I panicked. And I said some really shitty things. I don't fucking care if you can't afford some big fancy house in some hoity-toity neighborhood, and neither does Ainsley. She's never cared about that. I was the one who wanted out. I was the one who wanted more."

"And you can still have it," I tell him. "Finn, you're twenty-six years old. You still have your entire life ahead of you. If you want more, the only person standing in your way is you."

"I guess." He shuffles his feet, looking down at his sister. "I just always wanted her to be taken care of, you know? I wanted to protect her from anyone or anything that could potentially hurt her."

"Including me," I interject, pulling his gaze back to me. "Look, I get it. Just because I've looked out for you and Ainsley doesn't mean I'm this perfect man. I'm certainly not a man that deserves someone like her." It's my turn to look down at Ainsley. Her stapled head. Her bruised face. Her pale complexion. It feels like someone is sticking a white-hot branding iron straight down my throat, burning me from the inside out.

"You are exactly the kind of man that Ainsley needs and deserves." I look back up to find him watching me. "Ainsley doesn't need a *perfect* man. She needs someone that will fight for her. That will defend her. That will stand by her. That will put her before himself, *always*. I can't think of one single person on this Earth more equipped to do that than you. And she loves you. Hell, I think maybe she's always loved you. It's not my place to stand in the way of you two being together, and quite frankly, I don't want to. Seeing you two happy means more to me than anything else."

"I don't know what to say."

"Say you'll love her no matter what life throws your way. Say you'll take care of her always. Say you'll never let anything like this happen to her ever again." He gives me a sad smile. "Promise me that she will always be safe with you."

"I promise."

"Then you have my blessing. Not that you ever actually needed it."

"You're sure?"

"Is she who you want?"

"More than I've ever wanted anything in my life," I answer with complete honesty.

"Then yes, I'm sure." He nods. "I'm not saying it won't take some getting used to. Seeing you two together."

"I expect that it will." I chuckle.

"But I think it's time I take a step back and let Ainsley make her own choices."

"And maybe time for you to move forward with your life as well," I tell him. "You got the new job. Maybe now you make things right with your girl."

"I was awful to her. If it wasn't for us trying to find Ainsley she probably still wouldn't be speaking to me. I'd be lying if I said I didn't deserve it. She deserves better than I gave her."

"Then apologize. No one's perfect. You're allowed to fuck up from time to time. It's about what you do next that matters."

"Fuck you." He grins. "I swear, prison made you smart or something. You never used to talk like this before. In fact, you probably would bust my balls for even mentioning feelings."

"In my defense, we were young and stupid back then. I like to think I've matured with age. Maybe you should try it sometime."

"Ha. Ha." He flips me off.

"Would you two shut the hell up?" We both look down at Ainsley, my heart nearly leaping out of my chest.

Both of her eyes are open but she's not looking at either of us. She blinks once, then twice, before her gaze finally finds mine.

"You're awake." I smile, the rush of relief that overtakes me is so intense it causes tears to fill my eyes.

"Where am I?" She squeezes my hand when I slide mine into her uninjured one.

"You're in the hospital," Finn answers, pulling her attention to him. "We'll explain everything soon, but first I need to get the doctor." With that, he spins around and quickly jogs out of the room.

"Ryland?" She looks up at me, her eyes full of question.

"Don't worry," I tell her, leaning down. "You're safe. That's all that matters." I gently rest my forehead against hers, careful not to put any pressure on her. "I love you, Ainsley. I'm so sorry it took me until now to say it." I press a soft kiss to her lips before pulling back.

"You love me?" She gives me a crooked smile and I realize she's probably feeling the effects of the pain medication they've been pumping into her IV all day.

"I do."

"Say it again." Her eyes flutter closed.

"I love you," I repeat, watching her smile reappear moments before her eyes reopen.

"I love you, too." Her eyes close again and I can't help but wonder if she'll remember a second of this conversation. Not that it really matters because telling her I love her is something I plan to do a million more times. I'm going to say it so much that eventually she's going to be sick of hearing it. And then I'm going to say it some more.

Ainsley has always been my reason for living. From the time she was just a little girl I knew there wasn't a thing in this world I wouldn't do for her. She gave me something to fight for. Something to protect. Something to keep me straight when the whole world threatened to throw me off track.

I've loved her in some capacity since the day she was born. And while I may have never expected that love to morph into what it is today, nothing has ever felt more right in my entire life.

Chapter 27

Ainsley

"Careful," Finn says, watching Ryland help me out of the car like I'm some fragile piece of glass that's going to shatter if anything touches me.

It's how he's been treating me since this whole ordeal happened. And while I understand why he's acting this way, I wish he'd realize that I'm stronger than I look.

When I woke up in the hospital nine days ago, I had no recollection of the events that had taken place. But slowly my memory started to return, and with it, the reminder of how differently this whole situation could have turned out.

Thanks to Finn, Ryland, and Lily, my life didn't end along with Oscar's. The doctor said had they not found me when they did that I would have bled out within the hour. That's how close it came.

I had no idea when I flung myself at Oscar on that staircase the three of them were already on their way. Though I'm not sure that would have stopped me from doing what I did. I didn't set out to kill Oscar or myself. I just wanted to stop him from taking any more from me than he already had.

I'd do it all over again if I had to.

It wasn't until a few days ago that I learned what everyone else already knew. That Oscar had been home a lot longer than I knew. That he had flunked out of school and lost his baseball scholarship, and for some reason he felt I was to blame. His possessiveness over me had become an obsession and it became clear the night he kidnapped me that he was prepared to see it all the way through.

"I've got her." Ryland shakes his head at Finn as he guides me away from the car, kicking the door shut with his foot.

"I love you both, but if you two don't relax I'm going to go stay with Lily," I warn them, leaning into Ryland's side as he helps me up the front steps. "I'm perfectly capable of taking care of myself." Even though the truth is it's still difficult for me to get around. The injury to my abdomen was pretty severe and I still have a lot of healing to do.

"Trust me, that much we know is true." Ryland winks at me.

Despite all the pain and discomfort I feel physically, mentally I'm not sure I've ever felt more alive. What happened with Oscar made me realize a lot of things. The most important being that you can't take a single moment for granted. And from now on, I plan to cherish every minute I get. Especially the ones I get to share with Ryland.

I know it won't be an easy road. If the nightmares that have plagued my sleep nearly every night are any indication, I know I'm far from okay. But I also know eventually I will be.

I'm just so grateful that I'm still here. That Finn gave Ryland and me his blessing and that we actually have a real chance to be together. That I have the chance to finish school and see my dreams come true. That I get the chance to build the life I've always wanted. And that I get to do it all with the man I've loved since I was old enough to understand what loving someone meant.

Life doesn't always take the path of least resistance, but it has a funny way of spitting you out exactly where you're meant to be. And I have no doubt that here, with Ryland, is where I belong. It's where I've always belonged.

"You coming, slow poke?" Finn teases from the porch, holding the front door open for me.

"Careful," I warn. "I might be slow but I can still stab you in your sleep."

Ryland goes ramrod straight next to me at the same moment Finn's expression pales.

"What?" I ask, looking between the two of them. "Too soon?"

"You have a sick sense of humor." Finn shakes his head, stepping to the side so that Ryland and I can pass.

"Well if you can't learn to laugh at the bad shit that happens then you'll never find much joy in this life," I repeat the phrase our dad used to always say. It never made much sense to me as a kid, but now I see the wisdom behind his words. Because it's true.

"Surprise!" Lily squeals right as I step through the front door into the living room.

I jump slightly and immediately cringe, the pain in my abdomen shooting all the way to my toes.

"Oh shit, Ains. I'm sorry."

I look back up, seeing the *Welcome Home* banner and the multiple balloon bouquets behind her.

"That's okay." I force a smile through the pain. "What is all this?"

"It was Lily's idea." Ryland helps me further into the room and eases me onto the couch.

"I thought what better way for you to come home than to come home to all your favorite things," she sings, stepping in front of the coffee table. She waves her arms at the contents spread across the top. "We have your favorite pineapple pizza from Maggiano's." She opens the lid, the delicious aroma of garlic and cheese filling my nose. "We have red velvet cupcakes from your favorite bakery." She opens the white pastry box and my mouth practically waters. "And…" she draws out. "Drum roll, please." She beats her hands on the tops of her legs.

"We have this." Finn appears by her side, a plastic grocery bag in his hands. Without another word, he tips it upside down and several movies come tumbling out.

"Every single season of *The Big Bang Theory*." Lily smiles, clearly pleased with herself. "We figured if you were going to be laid up for a while it might be nice to have something to watch."

"You guys." I look at my best friend and my brother before glancing to the side where Ryland has taken the seat next to me. "You didn't have to do all this."

"We wanted to," Finn assured me. "We just wanted you to be able to come home and enjoy some of your favorite things. After everything you've been through, you deserve it."

"So does that mean everyone has reserved the rest of their afternoon and evening to overeating all this unhealthy goodness and binge-watching Sheldon Cooper with me?" I smile, once again looking around at all three of them.

"There's nowhere else we'd rather be." Ryland slides his hand into my un-casted one before lifting it to his mouth. He lays a light kiss to the back before resting our entwined fingers in his lap.

I've always known I was lucky. Lucky to have Finn for a brother. Lucky to have Lily for a friend. Lucky to have someone like Ryland in my life, even when I was trying to act like I hated him.

I may not have been blessed in all areas of my life, but right now, sitting here with my three favorite people in the entire world, I can't help but feel anything but extremely grateful.

To be here. To be alive. To have all of them in my life. Sometimes it takes thinking you've lost everything to realize just how much you truly stand to lose.

"Well then, what are you waiting for?" I smile up at Lily. She claps her hands together, snagging season one off the table before making quick work of slipping it into the Blu-Ray player.

I settle back against Ryland, turning my face up to meet his gaze. "I love you," I mouth so no one else can hear.

"I love you, too." He smiles, leaning down to lay a soft kiss to my lips.

"Oh for fuck's sake," Finn groans. I laugh against Ryland's mouth before turning my attention to my brother. "I said I was okay with you two being a couple. I never said it was okay to do that shit in front of me." He gestures between the two of us.

"Sit down." Lily appears at his side, shoving him into the armchair before plopping down on his lap. "You leave them alone." She playfully smacks his arm.

"How am I supposed to eat pizza if you're sitting on top of me?" He gives her an amused look.

"Guess you'll have to use your imagination." She drapes her legs over his lap.

It's strange how we all ended up here. Lily and Finn. Me and Ryland. It feels like only yesterday we were all living a different version of this life. Lily and Finn barely knew each other. Ryland was still in jail. And I was numbly walking through life, trying to convince myself that I was happy.

And now here we are. All connected. Our lives intertwining into one weird and crazy version of a family. And as hard as the road was to get here, I'd do it all over again if it meant I'd end up right back here.

While the people we love the most have the power to cut us the deepest, they are also the ones that make any of this worthwhile. And right now, I'm cherishing every single scar I've collected along the way. Because in the end, it's all been worth it.

Epilogue

Ryland

Eighteen Months Later...

"Ryland, are you home?" Ainsley calls as she walks through the front door.

Finn jumps to his feet and immediately heads for the backdoor.

"Where are you going?" I hiss at him, watching him slide his coat on.

"You asked for my blessing and I gave it. I'm not sticking around to watch." He chuckles. "Don't worry, it doesn't matter how you decide to ask. She loves you. There's no way she won't say yes." He gives me a reassuring smile before turning and slipping out the back door right as Ainsley enters the kitchen.

"Was that Finn?" she asks, gesturing toward the door as she kicks off her shoes and removes her coat.

"Yeah, he had to get home. Apparently Lily's morning sickness has turned into evening sickness. Well, all day sickness really," I say, stepping in front of her seconds before pulling her into my arms.

I give her a soft kiss before pulling back to look down at her pretty face. Even with messy hair and cheeks red from the wind, she's still the most beautiful thing I've ever laid eyes on.

"I still can't believe Lily and Finn are going to be parents." She giggles, stepping out of my embrace.

"I told you the minute we moved out and left those two alone they'd start reproducing." I smack her backside when she steps past me toward the refrigerator.

Honestly, I was more than a little surprised when Ainsley suggested we put an offer in on this house. She had just graduated college a couple months prior and had landed her first job with the county as a social worker. She was still trying to get her footing from being a student to a career woman. I didn't think it was good timing. But like most things, once Ainsley sets her mind to it, there's no convincing her otherwise. And like always, I caved with the first pouty lip she threw my way.

Even though I had my reservations about getting a place of our own, I couldn't be happier that we did. Not only has it done us good to have our own space – the old house was a bit crowded with the four of us living there – it's also been nice getting out from under Finn. As accepting as he's been, Ainsley is still his little sister and having him step in every time we had a small disagreement was not good for anyone involved.

Not to mention this house is perfect for us. It's in an up and coming neighborhood, so we got a really good price and it's only fifteen minutes from Finn and Lily, which I know was important to Ainsley. It's also close to both of our jobs.

I started working for a rehabilitation program that helps newly released convicts find housing and work about two months ago, and it has been more than I could have ever asked for. The office is right around the corner from Ainsley's so it gives me an excuse to stop by and have lunch with her when she has time.

"Is that your way of saying it's my fault?" Ainsley snorts, leaning against the refrigerator door as she browses over the contents inside. "What are you thinking for dinner? We have the stuff to make tacos. Or," she pauses, "I could whip up some pancake batter and we could have breakfast for dinner."

"Actually." I clear my throat, prompting her to turn back toward me. "I was thinking maybe we could head over to Apollo's."

"Apollo's? We haven't been there in ages."

"I know. And since it's *our* place, I thought maybe that's where we could go to celebrate."

I hadn't planned on doing this *now*. Hell, I just bought the ring *and* talked to Finn today. But seeing her standing here, in our kitchen, so beautiful that she nearly takes my breath away, I see absolutely no reason to wait.

"And what are we celebrating?" she asks, cocking her head to the side.

"Well, I'm hoping we're going to be celebrating you agreeing to be my wife."

With that, I drop to one knee, holding out the ring box I was hiding behind my back.

"Ryland." She gasps, looking so caught off guard you would think she had no idea this was coming.

How could she not? She's had me wrapped around her little finger since the day she was born. It shouldn't surprise her that all these years later I want to marry her.

"I'm not prince charming. I don't have a horse or a castle. I can't promise you that everything will always be perfect. It won't be. I'll mess up, like I often do. And you'll forgive me, because that's the amazing woman you are. What I can promise you is that I will love you deeper and more passionately than any man has ever loved a woman. I will stand by you. I will support you. And I will cherish every single day we get together on this Earth. I don't have anything to offer you… except myself." I smile up at her. "And I'm hoping that's enough." With that, I pop open the ring box. "Ainsley Marie Kenter, will you marry me?"

I barely get the question out before Ainsley is in my arms. She nearly tackles me to the ground, but I'm able to balance myself just in the nick of time.

"Yes!" she cries out, happy tears streaming down her face as I lift us both to our feet. "Yes," she repeats once she has a chance to compose herself. "I love you." She takes my face in both her hands.

"I love you, too. So much. I don't know what I did to deserve you, but I swear I'll spend the rest of my life proving to you that you made the right decision in choosing me."

"There was never a choice. It's always been you." She kisses me once more before stepping back to allow me to slide the modest ring onto her finger. She looks down at it for a brief moment before she's back in my arms, exactly where she belongs.

The End

Made in the USA
Middletown, DE
25 January 2020